"Linzi Jar[...] has a pleasant ring to it, which is something I find quite surprising."

"Surprising? Are you saying it contrasts with the owner?"

"I mean it contrasts with what I've heard about the owner," he admitted with a mirthless smile.

"Heard? What do you mean?"

But Guy did not enlighten her. Instead he said, "It's the sort of name some girls might not wish to change."

"Well, I have no intention of doing so."

His glance dropped to her ringless left hand. "Surely the day will come when you'll follow your aunt's example?"

"I doubt it," she returned in a cool tone.

"Then that makes two of us."

"Then I trust you'll keep yourself out of harm's way, Mr. Nelson. Don't be like your poor uncle and fall into the female trap."

"I'll take care." The words came grimly.

Miriam Macgregor has written eight books of historical non-fiction, but turned to romance in 1980. Many years on a sheep and cattle farm in New Zealand gave her an insight into rural life. She lived on the coast at Westshore, a suburb of Napier, where her desk overlooked Hawke Bay, a corner of the south Pacific Ocean, but she has since swapped the Pacific Ocean for the Atlantic and has emigrated to Middlesex, England. She enjoys painting in oils, watercolors and pastels, and does her own housework and gardening while planning her romantic novels.

The Best Man
for Linzi
Miriam Macgregor

Harlequin Books

TORONTO • NEW YORK • LONDON
AMSTERDAM • PARIS • SYDNEY • HAMBURG
STOCKHOLM • ATHENS • TOKYO • MILAN
MADRID • WARSAW • BUDAPEST • AUCKLAND

ISBN 0-373-17330-X

THE BEST MAN FOR LINZI

First North American Publication 1997.

CHAPTER ONE

LINZI JARDINE'S first encounter with Guy Nelson was at the wedding of her aunt, Beatrice White, to his uncle, Richard Nelson.

As he walked up the aisle behind the fifty-year-old bride who was her mother's younger sister, she was impressed by the handsome appearance of the man acting as best man to his equally tall and distinguished-looking relative. Her interest quickened as she realised he was a younger version of Richard, but as their glances met she was not prepared for the look of contempt that was flashed towards her.

Linzi felt shocked. She was not in the habit of receiving hostile glances from men. Therefore she told herself that she'd been mistaken. Or that it had been her imagination. However, she knew it was neither.

She also knew that she had never met this man before, and in fact had not yet even been introduced to him—so why that look of disdain? Then, shrugging the question aside, she put her mind to her bridesmaid duties. She was here to support the bride rather than concern herself about the best man.

The small church at Thames, situated at the base of New Zealand's Coromandel Peninsula, was filled with friends and relatives dressed in summer attire to cope with the heat of January in the Southern hemisphere. And as the words of the marriage service echoed between the walls Linzi found herself flicking veiled glances at the regular features of the best man's profile.

She noted the straight nose, the hard line of the jaw and the jut of the determined chin. His thick dark hair was well groomed, but she was aware that after the first brief look of derision his hazel eyes, set beneath black brows, had continued to ignore her.

5

So this was Guy Nelson, a man who for reasons of his own appeared to disapprove of her. The thought gave her an inward smile while she recalled the recent conversation with her aunt. And as the ceremony progressed her memory wafted beyond the vicar's voice to their last few minutes in the bedroom at her parents' home.

Linzi's blue-green eyes had been full of affection as they had regarded the older woman in her elegant cream dress trimmed with turquoise, a colour which was repeated in her matching hat. 'You look lovely, Aunt Bea!' she had exclaimed. 'Love suits you. When we reach the altar Richard will be bowled over backwards.'

Beatrice had given a rueful laugh. 'I know exactly how being fifty makes me look—mainly that I'm not to be compared with you. That floating turquoise fabric makes you look like a wood-nymph. Your eyes reflect it exactly, and the colour looks wonderful with your wavy auburn hair. Guy is the one who will be bowled over backwards. Just you wait and see...'

But Guy had not been bowled over. He had not dropped to the floor in a fit of ecstatic admiration. Quite the reverse in fact, and again she wondered why the one glance he had bestowed upon her had been filled with such blatant antagonism.

Her thoughts flew back to the bedroom, where Bea had said anxiously, 'I hope Guy will get here on time. He has to drive from Auckland, and that's seventy miles from Thames.'

Linzi had smiled, 'Then it's just as well you're not getting married in Coromandel, because that's another thirty miles along the coast road.'

Bea had sighed. 'After living there for all these years I can't believe I'm leaving my old home to live at Thames...but of course Richard's business is here, and Coromandel is a little too far away.' She had paused as a thought had struck her. 'Linzi, dear, I want a painting of that cottage...and one of the pohutukawa tree near the beach. You remember the old gnarled one that leans over the sand? Perhaps a boat on the beach would give added interest in the foreground. Could you do them while we're away on our honeymoon?' Bea's voice had held a pleading note.

'I'd have to stay in the cottage,' Linzi had pointed out.

'Of course.' Bea had opened her handbag. 'Here's the key to the back door. Take it now in case I forget to give it to you later.'

Linzi had felt a surge of enthusiasm. 'I could do a few extra paintings for my exhibition. I suppose you know I'm working towards a collection for an exhibition?'

'That's a good idea, and it's high time you had a showing,' Bea had said. 'But don't you dare sell the cottage or the tree to anyone but me.'

Linzi had laughed. 'Nonsense. They can be my wedding present to you and Richard. I've been wondering what to give a couple who appear to have everything, and now the problem is solved.'

'Richard will be delighted. He likes your work. He says you make a tree look like its own special species. And he loves Kauri Cottage. It's where we found each other,' Bea had admitted without the slighest trace of embarrassment. 'It's been our cottage of contentment.'

Linzi had made no comment. She knew that Richard had spent numerous weekends with her widowed aunt. Nor had she imagined their relationship to be purely platonic. The radiance in her aunt's face had told its own story, and Linzi felt happy for her.

And now, shaking herself mentally, she dragged her thoughts back to the present, but despite herself she was unable to prevent further surreptitious glances from sliding towards the best man. There was an aura of vitality about him, she thought. His athletic form indicated muscular strength beneath the immaculate, well-cut suit, and she found herself wondering about the way his mind worked.

Vaguely intrigued despite his unfriendly attitude, she became conscious of a sudden desire to know more about him, then chided herself for being a fool. He's probably married, or at least engaged to some gorgeous blonde, she decided.

That was the reason he hadn't been rushing from Auckland to visit his uncle at Thames—which was why she hadn't seen him before today, and why she knew absolutely nothing about him. And as she continued secretly to study his attractive profile she guessed his age to be in the early thirties—perhaps about seven years older than her own twenty-three years.

Moments later his touch on her arm sent a tremor shooting along her nerves. She turned to find the hazel eyes regarding her with a remote chilliness, but when he spoke his voice had a depth of timbre that was pleasing to her ears.

'You and I are expected to sign the register as witnesses,' he pointed out without even the vaguest hint of a smile.

'Oh. . .yes. . .of course.' She gathered her wits into some semblance of order while allowing herself to be drawn towards a table set aside from the altar. On it lay a large, open book. Her hand was not quite as steady as she would have wished, but she drew a deep breath and wrote her name in the place indicated.

The man beside her stared at the neat signature then spoke in a low tone, his words almost drowned by the sound of rising organ music. 'Linzi Jardine. . . The name has a pleasant ring to it, which is something I find quite surprising.'

Nettled, she stared at him blankly. 'Surprising? Are you saying it contrasts with the owner?' she demanded, while hoping that her inner hurt didn't show on her face.

'I mean it contrasts with what I've heard about the owner,' he admitted with a mirthless smile.

Her indignation grew. '*Heard?* What do you mean?'

But he did not enlighten her. Instead he said, 'It's the sort of name some girls might wish to change.'

'Indeed? Well, I have no intention of doing so.'

His glance dropped to her ringless left hand. 'Surely the day will come when you'll follow your aunt's example?'

'I doubt it,' she returned in a cool tone. 'I have much work to do and I prefer to remain free to get on with it.'

'Then that makes two of us,' he retorted with a grin that wiped the serious expression from his face. 'Work can't be done well with an encumbrance attached.'

Puzzled, she tried to fathom his meaning but was forced to ask, 'What do you mean by "encumbrance"?'

The broad shoulders lifted in a slight shrug. 'Oh. . . anything that drags the mind away from the main project of one's work.' His eyes rested momentarily on the soft waves of her shoulder-length auburn hair with its small floral decoration, then his sensuous mouth twisted slightly as he added, 'The female of the species can be a major offender when it comes to being an encumbrance.'

'Then I trust you'll keep yourself out of harm's way, Mr Nelson. Don't be like your poor uncle and fall into the female trap.'

'I'll take care.' The words came grimly.

She spoke with studied sweetness. 'I presume you have neither a wife nor a fiancée among the guests?'

'Nor anywhere else, thank you very much.'

Further conversation was impossible because moments later they were following the newly married couple down the aisle to the strains of the 'Wedding March'. Linzi took Guy's arm because it seemed to be expected of her, but she did so while bristling with irritation. This man was chauvinistic to the eyeballs, she decided crossly.

But suddenly her thoughts were sent whirling in a different direction, causing her steps to falter as she saw two people at the end of one of the pews. *Garth and Brenda Shaw*, she realised with a sense of shock. Who on earth had invited *them* to this wedding? Certainly not her aunt. In which case the invitation must have come from Richard's side.

Linzi had no wish to come in contact with Garth Shaw again—*ever*. And now the tall, sandy-haired man looked at her with a mocking smile, while Brenda ignored her.

But Brenda did not ignore Guy. Her dark eyes glowed as they rested upon him, while her hand reaching out caused him to pause. 'Guy. . .' she breathed. 'We must talk some more—'

'I'll see you outside the church,' he responded as he and Linzi moved on.

Linzi spoke in a casual tone. 'They must be friends of your uncle.'

'Actually, Brenda is a very old friend of mine. Richard thought I might like to see her again, and I had a chat with her before coming into the church.' His tone hardened as he added significantly, 'She confided a few of her troubles to me.'

Linzi's smile was full of understanding. 'I'll bet she has a few.'

'You should know,' he retorted drily.

'I beg your pardon?' Her head jerked round as she stared at him frostily. Was this something to do with his previous hostility?

He made no reply, and as others followed them from the church he drew her towards friends clustering round the bride and groom. There was much chatter and laughter filling the air while photographers became busy, and a short time later he ushered her into the passenger seat of a rakish red sports Toyota Supra.

As they drove towards the restaurant where the reception was to be held she pondered pursuing the subject, then decided against it. She had no wish to discuss Brenda's problems, especially as the sight of Garth had almost ruined her day. However, he was still nagging at her mind when Guy spoke abruptly.

'This work you mentioned—what is it?'

Thankful for the change of subject, she said, 'I'm a picture framer. I have a business in Thames.'

His brows shot up as his voice echoed his surprise. 'Good grief, isn't that rather odd employment for a girl?'

She stared straight ahead. 'It suits me.' There was no need to tell him it enabled her to frame her own paintings, she decided, and even less need to tell him she'd learnt the trade from Garth Shaw. To begin talking about it would bring back the days when she'd worked for him. It would remind her of the sexual harassment she'd had to endure, and how, despite her protests, she'd had difficulty holding him at arm's length. It was all something she wished to forget, especially on a day such as this.

Eventually she had confided the problem to her father, who had regarded her thoughtfully until he'd said, 'Why not beat him at his own job? How would you like to be set up in your own business? I'll back you financially.'

At first the fear of risking her father's money had filled her with apprehension, although the more she'd thought about it, the more she'd realised that most of their customers preferred her choice of frames and mounts to Garth's.

And then the day had come when her employer had really overstepped the mark—by forcing her into a corner, kissing and mauling her, while holding her in a grip from which she had found it hard to struggle free. When she had finally managed to, she had rushed out of the shop, never to return.

And now, recalling the incident, she realised that it had all happened for the best, because without it she would not now be enjoying the success of her own business. Most of Garth's customers had followed her, and the debt to her father had long since been repaid.

Guy's voice cut across her memories. 'You've become very quiet. Does something trouble you?'

'No, why should it?' No way would she reveal those thoughts.

'I thought Shaw looked at you in a peculiar manner. You obviously know each other.' He sent her a side-glance with one dark brow raised, while his tone hinted at irony.

He's perceptive, she thought, then made an effort to keep her voice calm. 'I used to work for him,' she admitted, knowing that Brenda would acquaint him with this fact; then she found herself saying, 'He didn't look at me in the same manner that Brenda gazed at you.'

He was silent for several long moments before he said, 'There was a time when we were fairly close. And then she met Garth Shaw.' The words ended with a trace of bitterness.

'You're still fond of her?' Linzi asked gently.

He seemed to consider the question, then said, 'Our parents lived near each other. We went to school together and grew up seeing each other daily. It was really a boy-and-girl affair that began when she brought all her troubles to me, which was something that boosted my ego. I suppose I'll always have a soft spot for Brenda.'

The answer did not really tell Linzi what she wanted to know; then she frowned, wondering why this man's feelings for Brenda Shaw should hold any interest for her.

Unexpectedly, he said, 'Life with Shaw hasn't been easy for Brenda. He has a roving eye.'

And wandering hands, Linzi could have informed the man beside her, but she merely said, 'Oh, is that a fact?'

He sent her a swift glance. 'Don't tell me you're unaware of his little habits?'

'I wasn't with him for very long before I realised it would be wiser for me to leave,' she said evasively and with truth, then feared he might ask for further details.

But he did not. Instead he said, 'I've told Brenda

she'd be wise to dump Shaw. Toss him back onto the open market for whoever has an eye for him.' The words were accompanied by another side-glance towards Linzi.

She said nothing, although she had a strong suspicion that the statement implied more than it said.

He went on, 'I consider Brenda deserved better than Shaw. I've also told her she should make a fresh start by finding herself a man with integrity.'

Linzi's voice became sweet as she turned to look at him reflectively. 'I believe you're more fond of her than you care to admit. Were you badly hurt when she married Garth Shaw?'

His jaw tightened as he retorted harshly, 'I said it was a boy-and-girl affair. Do you mind if we drop the subject? It's not one that I'm mad about discussing.'

She smiled. 'OK, I've got the message. Obviously it's a sore point with you.' He must have been really hurt by Brenda's marriage, she decided, feeling an unexpected sympathy for him.

His voice still vaguely annoyed, he said, 'Suppose you guide me to this country house where the reception is to be held. It's years since I've been in Thames and I'm not sure of the turning.'

After that Linzi directed him to follow the highway running north of the town. On their left the sparkling blue waters of the Firth of Thames lapped the shores where the twisted trunks and branches of pohutukawa trees supported large clusters of crimson blossoms. Known as the New Zealand Christmas trees, they never failed to fascinate her, and she thought of the one near the cottage at Coromandel that she would later paint for her aunt.

On their right the land rose towards the forest-covered mountain range which divided the peninsula like a long blue backbone. The road turned towards it, winding uphill until it reached a large timber-built house in an elevated position that offered views of the extensive coastal district.

At one time it had been the private home of a prosperous early settler. Its sides and back were surrounded by a bush area of trees, while the front featured well-kept lawns and gardens that were bright with flowers. And although Linzi had been to this place for other receptions she never failed to take pleasure in walking along its woodland paths.

Guy parked the car on a large paved area, and as they walked towards the house Brenda came out to the veranda. It was almost as though she had been awaiting their arrival. There was no sign of Garth, and Linzi suspected that he was already at the bar. Even when she had been working for him, Garth had been too fond of whisky.

As they approached the top of the wide concrete steps the dark-haired woman stepped forward to clutch at Guy's arm, and again the dark eyes glowed as they gazed up into his face. 'Guy, I *must* speak to you. I'm sure Miss Jardine will excuse us,' she added with a hint of dismissal in her tone.

'Of course.' Linzi forced a smile and went into the reception room where somebody put a glass of sparkling pale gold liquid into her hand.

She felt more than a little irritated by the high-handed manner in which Brenda had commandeered Guy's attention, but, as he had said, they were old friends, and she now realised they were both about the same age. Nevertheless, there was something about the intensity of Brenda's attitude that puzzled her, and despite herself she was drawn towards the large window at the end of the reception room.

Through it she could see that Brenda had coaxed Guy towards the end of the veranda where they could talk privately. She appeared to be speaking earnestly, and as he listened a scowl became settled on his face. Was she herself the subject of their discussion? Linzi wondered. An uncomfortable feeling came over her as instinct warned that this was so. Nor was it difficult to guess the trend of Brenda's complaints.

And then Garth Shaw's mocking drawl came from behind her. 'Hello, beautiful—fancy seeing you standing at the altar beside his lordship. Did you wish you were both taking the place of the bride and groom? You'd be unwise to set your sights on him. I know someone who has done so without success.'

Curiosity made her say, 'You mean Brenda?'

'Of course. So I'm warning you. . .he's a wily bird and not to be caught.' His pale blue eyes glinted at her.

Memory of Guy's words about not wanting to be encumbered made her say, 'His wish to remain free is no problem to me. Now will you please go away? I've no desire to talk to you. We have nothing to say to each other.'

'Does that mean I'm still unforgiven for stealing a kiss?'

'*Definitely*. And for everything else you had in mind.'

'Then that makes us quits, because I haven't forgiven you.'

She stared at him loftily, not deigning to ask what he meant.

'You stole most of my customers,' he explained, his mouth giving an angry twist. 'However, I'll admit you always had a good eye for frames and mounts and colour. That bluish-green dress suits you. What is it—blue or green? It makes your eyes look like a pair of highly polished turquoise gems.'

'Thank you, I don't need your compliments. You should keep them for Brenda,' Linzi said, longing to be rid of him.

'Brenda knows me and all my faults. She loves me after a fashion. . .at least next to somebody else,' he added gloomily, his eyes turning to where his wife stood talking with Guy. Then he frowned. 'What's she going on about now, I wonder?'

'Why don't you join them and find out?' Linzi suggested acidly.

Garth shrugged. 'I'd rather go and find another drink.'

'You do that if it's important,' Linzi snapped, feeling irritated because his attitude towards his wife appeared to be so casual. Garth Shaw, she decided, was enough to put a girl off all men. . .although surely all men were not like Garth Shaw? Staring into her glass, she was still pondering the question when Guy came to her side.

Golden sparks glinted in the hazel eyes, while his voice had an edge to it. 'Shaw has been showering you with his usual charm?'

'I didn't know he had any,' she returned, realising that Guy must have seen them together.

His tone became even more clipped. 'Brenda fears she's on the verge of a nervous breakdown. You wouldn't know anything about that, I suppose?'

'No. Brenda is a person with whom I have had little contact.'

'But you do have contact with her husband,' he stated coldly.

Her eyes widened. 'Not if I can help it.'

He gave a hiss of impatience, then gritted, 'Don't give me that innocent look. I understand you're having an affair with Shaw.'

Fury sent colour flooding into Linzi's face. 'That's a lie,' she ranted. 'How dare she say such a thing—'

He cut in, 'When Brenda and I talked before the wedding she told me of your activities with him, and now she has told me even more.'

Enlightenment dawned upon Linzi. 'Ah. . .now I understand.'

'What, may I ask, do you understand?' His voice had become bleak and his eyes moved from her auburn hair to the creaminess of her throat.

'The reason for your supercilious manner towards me at the altar. It's a wonder you didn't shout "Jezebel. . .Jezebel," during the ceremony.'

'It would have been appropriate?' he queried silkily.

'Certainly not,' she snapped, her chin raised. 'So, what else did your dear friend confide? Why not get it off your chest and be done with it? I'll answer whatever I can.' For some reason that she was unable to define she felt a strong urge to exonerate herself in this man's eyes.

He hesitated, frowning. 'I'm not in the habit of repeating conversations. It's not my style, but in this case it seems to be necessary.'

'So far you're doing very nicely,' she commented with derision. 'I might as well hear the rest.'

Guy's penetrating glare was relentless. 'Then perhaps you should know that I've been told you left Shaw's employ because you feared he would never divorce Brenda for you—'

'Utter damned rot,' she cut in furiously.

'Therefore you set up in opposition to punish him.'

Linzi's jaw sagged while she tried to keep a grip on the rage that threatened to overwhelm her. She longed to rush at Brenda while shouting the truth of the situation, but now was neither the time nor the place to do so. Then taking a deep breath, it was only with an effort that she was able to say, 'The poor woman— She must feel dreadfully insecure.'

'That's right. So what have you to say?' The words came as a challenge from between tight lips.

'You're waiting for me to vindicate myself, Mr Nelson?' she demanded haughtily.

'It would relieve me to know that Brenda has no further opposition to fear from you.' The words were gritted coldly.

She sent him a level glance, becoming conscious of a wave of perversity. 'Why? What has it got to do with you?'

'Just the fact that we're old friends, as I've already explained.'

'I see.' It had nothing to do with herself, she realised. He couldn't care less about where her own interests lay, so long as they weren't pointed in the direction of Garth Shaw. Nor was there any suggestion of his being concerned about her own integrity because obviously she meant nothing to him.

However, the desire to speak in her own defence got the better of her, and she asserted in a low voice, 'For your information, Mr Nelson, if Garth Shaw ever lays his hands on me again he'll get such a smack in the eye he'll wonder what's hit him. Is that sufficient to calm your fears on Brenda's behalf?'

'I hope so,' he assured her seriously. 'So long as you mean it.'

She glanced about the room, which was now crowded, then said with as much dignity as she could muster, 'People are beginning to find their places at tables. Shouldn't we be with the bride and groom? It's what we're here for—in case you've forgotten.'

'I'm unlikely to forget this day,' he returned in an undertone.

'Because it's a day when you've seen Brenda again?' The question just slipped out.

'Brenda belongs to another man and he belongs to her, which is something *you're* in the habit of forgetting,' he rasped.

Her limp trembled slightly as she recognised the blaze of accusation in his eyes. And, while she hated the fact that he should continue to regard her in this manner, she feared he'd be a hard man to convince that he was believing the wrong story.

Tears pricked her lids, causing her to turn and hasten to where her aunt was already seated beside Richard at the table. She knew that Guy followed to take his place beside his uncle, and she was thankful to be separated from him by the newly married couple.

Soon the wedding breakfast was served. Speeches were made, glasses were raised in toasts, and the white wedding cake was cut. Later, as the afternoon progressed, the bride and groom retired to changing rooms provided for the purpose.

Linzi followed her aunt into the bride's room, where she took charge of the hat and dress that Bea discarded, and as she gathered various other articles to store in the suitcase she heard the low murmur of men's voices through the wall.

The sound caused Bea to whisper, 'Richard and Guy are in the next room. My dear, I'm so glad you've met Guy. Richard tells me he's such a fine, steadfast young man. . .and I've heard he's *most* eligible.'

Linzi smiled. 'That's important, is it, Aunt?'

'Of course—but there must be love attached as well,' Bea said without hesitation, then changed the subject abruptly. 'Now then. . .you won't forget my cottage and tree paintings?'

'When you return you'll find them among the wedding gifts,' Linzi promised, hoping that this would be a fact.

When the bride and groom emerged they were ready to leave for their honeymoon. Guests crowded about Richard's car to see them off, and as Bea was about to step into the vehicle she turned and threw her bridal bouquet straight at Linzi.

Linzi caught it automatically, and as she did so the guests applauded while laughing teasingly. 'The next bride. . . You'll be the next bride. . . It's a sure sign!' many exclaimed.

Their words caused Linzi to blush. She wished she hadn't been so quick to catch the bouquet, but her action had been instinctive and without thought. 'I *won't*,' she protested.

'Oh, *yes*, you *will*,' the voices chorused in unison.

Guy spoke in her ear, his words unheard by people nearby because of the noise. 'You'll have to make sure the man is *free*—or have you already made a decision, despite your previous denials concerning Shaw?'

Linzi gasped as his meaning registered with her. She felt herself tremble with anger, and even as she raked her mind for a reply Garth's voice, slurred from too much drink, came thickly.

'You're all per-perfectly right. Linzi—hic—Linzi

won't be alone for long. She's got a man lined up. . .
Shomewhere. . .' The words ended in an inane giggle.

Little notice was taken of him, although Linzi
became aware of the manner in which Guy's eyes
continued to move from Garth to herself. His acute
observation did nothing to remove her frustration or to
calm her troubled state of mind, and suddenly she felt
unable to chat amicably with the guests who were
returning to the reception room. Nor did she wish to
hold the bouquet, so she placed it gently on the
concrete step.

She longed to be alone, to take in great gulps of
fresh air to soothe her ruffled emotions, and with
solitude in mind she set off across the lawn towards a
path that would take her to where the kauri trees rose
from a floor covered in ferns and undergrowth. Rising
to a hundred and fifty feet, their lofty, straight trunks
were branchless to a considerable height, and in the
silence that was such a blessed contrast to the laughter
and chatter of the reception room Linzi felt as though
she was walking between the columns of a cathedral.

She breathed deeply to soak in the tranquillity of the
idyllic surroundings, and as she examined the delicate
ferns growing along the edge of the path her own
irritations seemed to vanish. . .until the sound of a
voice brought them surging back.

'Hi, Linzi. . .wait for me.'

She froze, then turned slowly to see Garth coming
towards her, his unsteady gait causing him to weave
from one side of the track to the other. Annoyed, she
said, 'Please leave me alone.'

He leered at her. 'Come on, now. . .you knew I'd
follow you. It's why you came here.'

'Don't be ridiculous,' she snapped, then turned her
back and began to move rapidly along the path.

He staggered after her, 'Aw, gosh, Linzi, I—hic—
only want to talk to you. Can't we talk for a while?'

'No; I've nothing to say to you.' She began to run,

knowing it would be wiser to race ahead rather than to try and pass him to make her way back.

But her dainty, high-heeled turquoise sandals prevented her from being a match for the speed of his long legs, and despite his inebriated state he lunged forward, his fingers clawing at her arm and spinning her round to face him. 'You *will* talk to me,' he snarled.

She wrenched her arm free. '*No, I shall not*. And don't you dare lay your hands on me. . .'

He stared at her sullenly. 'Then hear thish. . . Brenda's been talking to hish lordship. . .about us. . .'

She glared at him coldly. 'I'm well aware of what has been said. How *dare* you tell her such lies about my reason for leaving the job?' Linzi's temper rose as she ranted at him furiously.

Garth's face became even more sullen. 'I ha-had to tell her—hic—a tale of shome sort. . .and I could hardly tell her the truth. She would have had my liver on a dish.'

'You craven, two-faced rat,' she spat at him. 'You make me sick.'

'Hell's teeth, I don't feel too good myself. . . I'm damned giddy.'

'Then I'll leave you to throw up. After that you'll feel better,' Linzi said, trying to edge past him.

'Don't leave me. . . I'm about to black out.' A hand went to his forehead while he swayed as though unable to remain standing.

Suddenly concerned, she stepped forward quickly, her hands grasping the lapels of his jacket in an effort to support him. But this was a mistake because the next instant she was clasped against his chest, held by arms like iron bands from which there was no escape.

'Shtraight into my arms, you little darling.' The words were mumbled above her head and an alcoholic belch escaped him.

Linzi decided against struggling. In Garth's unsteady state it would send them both crashing to the leaf-mould-covered path; therefore she thought quickly then grated through stiff lips, 'If you don't let me go I'll tell Brenda exactly why I left your employ.'

He dismissed the threat. 'I'll let you go when you've given me a kiss—a good, long, pr-proper one—hic—'

'I'll see you in hell first, you drunken idiot—'

Her words were cut short by the sardonic tones of a different voice that came from behind them. 'Well, well, well—a most touching scene if ever there was one.'

Dismayed, Linzi realised that Guy Nelson stood watching them from a short distance away, the disdain on his face more than obvious.

CHAPTER TWO

GARTH released Linzi as Guy came towards them. 'What d'you want?' he slurred belligerently.

Guy ignored him, his lip curling as his eyes raked Linzi with cold contempt. 'Not very fussy, are you?' he sneered. Then he rasped at Garth, 'Your *wife* has been searching for you, Shaw. I noticed Miss Jardine disappear through the opening in the bushes, so I knew where to find you both, even if it meant gatecrashing the rendezvous.'

'It was *not* a rendezvous,' Linzi protested wrathfully. She had felt a spasm of horror at being discovered in Garth's embrace, especially by this man, of all people, but was now thankful to be free of those arms. 'I came here for fresh air,' she asserted.

Garth smirked at her. 'You might as well try telling that to the birdish... You knew I'd follow you.'

Frustrated, she glared at him balefully. 'I did not. I'm not a mind-reader. Why don't you admit the truth of this stupid situation?'

Garth ran a hand through his sandy hair, then shrugged off the suggestion. 'I doubt that he'd believe me, after what he's just sheen.' The thought struck him as being funny, causing his inane giggle to emerge.

'Then try telling your wife the truth,' Linzi persisted angrily. She was feeling more upset than she cared to admit, even to herself.

'That's a good idea,' Guy agreed. 'Why don't you go and find Brenda? Tell her what you've been doing here. I'll vouch for it as an eyewitness.'

The other man scowled. 'You mind your own damned business. You needn't imagine I don't know you've always had a soft spot for Brenda.. just as she's always had one for you...' Then, making an effort to

23

straighten himself, he began to walk back to the old house.

Linzi noticed that his steps were now a little steadier, and she suspected that Guy's unexpected arrival had had a sobering effect on him. She was also aware that Guy stood regarding her with eyes that were icy cold.

'So, Brenda was right,' he gritted harshly. 'You *are* having an affair with her husband.'

Linzi stamped a foot. 'I am not!'

'Seeing is believing.'

'You saw nothing,' she lashed at him in fury. 'I thought he was about to fall. I was merely trying to hold him up when he. . .when he. . .'

'Took advantage of the open invitation?'

'That's right. But it wasn't an invitation—nor do I intend to discuss it with you,' she snapped angrily.

'Why not?'

'Because any explanation I make is likely to fall upon deaf ears, so why should I bother? In any case, your opinion of me matters not one iota,' she added loftily. But this, she knew, was a lie, and in an effort to sound convincing she said in a haughty tone, 'If you'll excuse me I'll continue with my walk. It's what I came here to do, rather than to meet *that man*, as you're so determined to believe.' She began to walk away but had gone only a few steps when his voice grated on her ears.

'I appear to have missed the highlight.' The words were drawled.

The sarcasm in his voice made her pause, then she turned slowly to face him. 'Highlight? What are you talking about?'

'Have you forgotten your own words?' There was a pause while he waited for her to respond, but when she continued to look at him blankly he went on to give a fair imitation of a female voice. "If Garth Shaw ever lays his hands on me again, he'll get such a smack in the eye he'll wonder what's hit him."' He paused again before adding ironically, 'I didn't notice it being delivered.'

'No? Then let me tell you there was something else you didn't notice,' she declared with her chin raised.

'Oh?' He sounded mildy interested. 'What would that have been?'

'The fact that I couldn't get my arms free. He had them pinned because I'd grabbed the lapels of his jacket to hold him up. . .but I've already told you that.'

'Well, he seemed to have recovered when he left. He didn't have to crawl, so he couldn't have been too bad,' Guy observed.

Frustrated, she glared at him wordlessly, then swung round and began to hasten along the track.

He kept pace with her. 'How far do you intend to go?'

She stared straight ahead while answering coolly, 'The track winds for a distance before it returns to the house. I'll do the round trip.'

His tone became mocking. 'Do you always take bush walks in such delicate footwear? There are sure to be damp places caused by springs. They're there, even in summer.'

She stood still to stare down at the sandals that matched her dress. In her haste to be alone she had forgotten about them, and already the leaf-mould was soiling them. If she went much further they'd be completely ruined. Only an idiot would traipse along this path in such flimsy footwear, she realised, and in this man's eyes she must already appear thoroughly stupid.

Stupid, as well as flirtatious enough to be casting eyes at another woman's husband, she thought. And again she tried to assure herself that she couldn't care less about his opinion of her. . .although deep down she knew that she did. Hadn't his remark during the bouquet incident upset her to the extent of sending her towards the solitude of this bushland track?

The thought brought her mind back to the matter of

her footwear. Ruefully she said, 'You're right about my shoes. I shouldn't be wearing them here. It was just that I felt a—a strong desire to get away from everybody.' A sigh betrayed her depression as she added, 'I'd better go back.'

'I'll carry you before further damage is done,' he offered.

She backed away from him. 'Oh, no. I can walk, thank you.' The thought of being carried by this man had an odd effect on her, and a gasp escaped her as she found herself being swung up into arms that felt as strong as steel.

He looked into her face, which was only a few inches below his own. 'No doubt you'd prefer Shaw's arms to mine.'

She glared at him then snapped, 'Certainly not— although I suspect you'd prefer to be carrying Brenda rather than myself.'

'What makes you so sure about that?' he demanded, striding along the path.

She spoke bitterly. 'It's because you're so quick to believe her without knowing the facts, and to accuse me without realising the truth. You don't even know the sort of person I am, yet you're so quick to judge me. . .' She bit her lip, annoyed with herself for having made this outburst.

He stared ahead, making no reply until they reached the opening that let them out onto the lawn. As he set her down on the grass a sardonic laugh escaped him. 'I can't imagine why my judgement of you should cause concern, especially as we're unlikely to meet again after today.'

'Which is something to be thankful for,' she said in a firm tone. But at the same time her blue-green eyes became shadowed by something more than her dark lashes as she realised that he had no wish to see her again. But what else could she expect? she asked herself dismally. And then the sound of departing cars caused them to turn towards the house.

Guy said, 'People are leaving. If you're ready I'll drive you home.'

Pride sent her chin a trifle higher. 'No, thank you. The wedding is over, so there's no need for you to bother about me any more. I'll find a lift with somebody else.'

His voice became clipped. 'You'll do nothing of the kind. It's the best man's duty to take care of the bridesmaid and I intend to see the job out. I brought you here and I'll take you home whether you like it or not.'

There was no mistaking the determination in his voice, and, secretly, Linzi felt relieved to be spared the embarrassment of having to search for a lift home. It would have meant admitting that she'd been left high and dry by this handsome man, thus giving the impression that she'd been unable to hold his interest for even a short time. Meekly she said, 'Thank you, I would be grateful.'

They walked to the house, where they collected the suitcases left by Richard and Bea, and as they went through the reception room Linzi was thankful not to be confronted by the Shaws. However, she noticed that Guy paused to look about him, and therefore said in a casual tone, 'Your friend has probably taken her inebriated husband home.'

His reply was little more than a grunt, and a few minutes later they were in the red Toyota and heading back towards the Thames township. When they reached the driveway of her parents' home he switched off the ignition, then sat looking at her.

She hesitated for a moment before taking the plunge by asking, 'Would you like to come in for coffee?'

He nodded affably. 'I thought you'd never ask.'

'To be honest, I felt sure you'd refuse.'

She led him into the house, then left him in the lounge while she went to the kitchen. On her return with two steaming mugs she found him examining a painting on the wall. It had her name on it, but he made no comment. Instead he said, 'Your parents weren't at the wedding. Why was that?'

'Because they're in Australia.'

He sipped his coffee thoughtfully, his eyes slightly narrowed as he asked, 'Why did they go away at this particular time? Was it because they disapproved of Bea marrying my uncle?'

'Good grief, that's a ridiculous suggestion.' Linzi stared at him wide-eyed as she went on, 'They both like Richard very much. They're really happy for Bea.'

'Yet they went on holiday instead of attending the wedding,' he pointed out with a hint of reproof.

'Who said they're on holiday?' Linzi demanded sharply. 'My goodness, you do jump to conclusions.'

'Then why aren't they here?' The question was snapped out. 'After all your mother is Bea's sister.'

She took a deep breath while controlling her impatience. This man was abrupt and to the point, she decided. He said what he thought without beating about the bush, but at least one knew where one stood with him. As for herself. . .she stood nowhere.

'Well?' he persisted, as though having difficulty in controlling his own impatience.

She forced a smile, determined to remain amicable. 'For your information, Mr Nelson, Gran, my father's mother, lives in Sydney. A few days ago she had a bad heart turn and they were called over there unexpectedly. Otherwise they would have been here. That's why we had to find somebody else to give Aunt Bea away.'

'I see. I didn't realise—'

'It's a wonder Richard didn't mention it.'

'He didn't have much opportunity. I arrived from Auckland with only a few minutes in which to get changed,' he explained.

Linzi was silent for several thoughtful moments before she said, 'I find you to be a very frank person, Mr Nelson. Do you mind if I ask you a frank question?'

'Of course not. Fire ahead—and for heaven's sake

call me Guy. I see no reason for this persistent formality.'

She ignored the latter request as she went on, 'For most of the day I've sensed you to be in a really cross mood, Mr Nelson. I can understand you being annoyed with me on account of what your friend Brenda told you, but is there also another reason. Is it possible you are also annoyed because of your uncle's marriage to my aunt?' Her eyes sent him a challenge.

He frowned. 'What on earth put that idea into your head?'

'It was just something Bea told me. She said you are Richard's only relative.'

'That's correct. So what?'

She saw his jaw tighten and sensed that he'd guessed her thoughts. She also knew she was on dangerous ground, and was already beginning to regret the question simmering in her mind, yet she continued bravely. 'I just wondered if you felt you were no longer his heir and were upset because of it. . .?' Her words trailed away as she watched his face darken with anger.

An oath escaped him as he rose from his chair and towered above her, a small muscle working in his cheek as he snarled, 'Hell's teeth, you've got a nerve. For your information, *Miss Jardine*, I'm more than financially independent of anything my uncle might leave behind, and, let me tell you, I don't know when I've been so damned insulted.'

She met his anger fearlessly. 'Then that makes us quits.'

'*Quits?* What the hell do you mean?'

'Do you think your own insulting assumption that I'm having an affair with Garth Shaw leaves me untouched?' she demanded quietly.

'I know only what Brenda has told me and what I saw for myself on the path,' he gritted at her. 'The latter scene spoke for itself.'

A sigh betrayed her frustration. 'I thought I'd explained what happened on the path. I'm sorry you don't believe me.' Her voice held a tremor as her eyes filled with tears which spilled over before she could stop them.

'Please don't turn on the waterworks,' he advised harshly. 'Crying will get you nowhere. It's not a weapon that has any effect on me.'

Furious with herself, she dabbed at her eyes then queried in a polite tone, 'Have you finished your coffee?'

'Yes. . .thank you.'

'Another mug?'

'No, thank you.' His mouth was a grim line.

'Then perhaps you'd better leave. I don't think we have anything further to say to each other—except that I'm sorry I made that suggestion about an inheritance. Even if it were true it's not my business.'

'You're dead right about that,' he rasped. 'I can't understand what put the idea into your head.'

'I *told* you—it was because you seemed to be so *cross*,' she reminded him. 'Especially with me, whom you'd only just met. I even sensed it at the altar, where it stuck out a mile.'

'The reason definitely escapes you?' he demanded tightly.

'Yes, of course it does.'

'Then let me spell it out. As I told you, Brenda's an old friend. It riles me to see the way in which you've hurt her. Is that clear enough?' His voice was hung with icicles.

'Quite clear,' she admitted from between stiff lips.

He went on, 'I'll admit I was feeling uptight when you came into the church. It was soon after I'd asked Brenda if she happened to know the bridesmaid. She gave me an earful.'

'And you believed her without question,' Linzi snapped wrathfully. 'Thank you very much.'

Guy's broad shoulders lifted in a slight shrug. 'Why would she lie to me? Anyway, as you said, we have nothing more to say to each other. Thank you for the coffee. I can see myself out. Goodbye.'

'Goodbye,' she muttered in a dull tone, watching him stride from the room. Then she listened for the bang of the front door, and although she had no wish for him to leave in this manner pride prevented her from running after him to placate and bring him back to talk more amicably.

'Goodbye'. The word had such a final ring about it. Would he also feel this and return of his own accord? She waited hopefully for the ring of the front doorbell, but it remained silent. Obviously, Guy Nelson had served his duty as best man to his uncle and he was finished with the bridesmaid. OK, so she would be finished with the best man.

The decision sent her to the bedroom where she slipped out of the turquoise dress and changed into a white blouse and dark green shorts that revealed her slim hips and long, beautifully shaped legs. She then carried the sandals to the laundry and with a listlessness that was foreign to her made an effort to remove the leaf-mould stains.

As she did so, and despite her recent vow, she was assailed by the memory of being lifted into Guy's arms and carried along the path. And now she had only to close her eyes to see the handsome features, the sensuous mouth that had been so close to her own. But of course she was the last person he'd have any desire to kiss.

'OK, Mr Nelson,' she said in vehement tones that echoed against the laundry walls. 'I shall forget you. I shall put you right out of my mind.'

But instead of doing so she again found herself continuing to wonder about him. Where had he gone when he'd stormed from the room? No doubt to his uncle's house, where he might be expected to spend the night before returning to Auckland. Or had he thrown his things into his bag and even now was on his way back to that city, the red Toyota sports car burning up the miles like a bright bullet?

If so, were the two suitcases still in the back of the car? And, even if he'd remembered to remove them, had he thought to open them and hang up the clothes? Perhaps she should phone to remind him to do so. At least it would give her the opportunity to hold out a cordial hand without losing too much face.

She went to the phone and pressed buttons, calling Richard's house, and heard the receiver lift immediately. It was almost as though Guy had been expecting it to ring, the gruffness of his deep voice indicating that he'd known it would be her.

It made her feel tempted to put the receiver down at once, but the thought of her aunt's expensive dress lying crushed in the suitcase made her say, 'Guy...? It's Linzi. I thought I'd better make sure you'll remember to hang up the clothes in the cases.'

'I did that as soon as I got inside the door.'

'Oh...then that's OK... Thank you.' She fell silent, waiting for him to say something further—something like, Are you doing anything this evening? But the question did not come; therefore she said in a small voice, 'Goodbye.'

'Goodbye.' The word came crisply.

She replaced the receiver. *Forget* him, you fool, she again told herself irately. Can't you see that he looks upon you with disdain, otherwise why would he snub you in this disgusting manner? And then anger boiled within her until she reminded herself to think about going to Coromandel where Kauri Cottage waited to be painted.

The reminder sent her out to her blue Fiat in the garage, and within a few minutes she had driven the short distance to where her studio was situated in one of the town's side-streets. It was divided into two sections, one being a painting area, the other a framing workshop where several watercolours by local artists waited to be framed.

The next few days saw her working steadily. The orders were completed and collected, and only then did she turn her attention to sorting out art materials to take to Coromandel. Oil paints and canvas boards were packed into the car, and near them, yet protected from any hint of oil, were blocks of stiff cartridge and watercolour paper. Her folding easel, with turpentine, linseed oil and rags, was safely stowed, and apart from her suitcase there was only a box of food to add to the collection.

By this time she was gripped by a sense of urgency. The days were passing and she knew that Richard and Aunt Bea would be away on their honeymoon for only a fortnight. It would be nice, she thought, to have the paintings of the cottage and the pohutukawa tree finished by their return, even if still unframed.

It was late in the afternoon when Linzi turned the car along the road that would take her to Coromandel. The sun was still warm, and for coolness she was again wearing her dark green shorts and white blouse. The sea breeze blowing in the open window brushed her wavy auburn hair from her face, and as she sped along she congratulated herself on having evicted Guy Nelson from her mind.

The road was one she never tired of travelling because it followed the coast for miles, the sea sparkling on her left, sending waves along to the roots of the pohutukawa trees lining that side of the highway. On her right rose coastal hills with settlements of holiday homes nestling against their tree-covered slopes.

Briefly, she wondered if she should have waited until morning before leaving, but she knew the road well and at this time of the year the long summer days would enable her to arrive before dark. But she had forgotten her habit of stopping the car to sketch a scene that happened to catch her eye, and by the time she had reached the Coromandel township and then

turned to drive over a hill and down to a bay dusk had
fallen.

Kauri Cottage was the last house on a road that
curved round the shore. A hill between it and the
nearest neighbouring houses meant that it was out of
sight and slightly isolated from the rest of the beach
community. Single-storeyed, it consisted of three bedrooms, a lounge, a dining room, a kitchen, a bathroom
and a laundry. Its steep gables over the windows
indicated that it had been built in earlier years, before
the long-lasting kauri timber had become so difficult to
obtain.

Linzi stopped the car at the entrance to the driveway
which swept round to the back of the house. It was
difficult to realise that Aunt Bea would not be inside
to welcome her, and for a few minutes she sat staring
at the white-painted walls and red roof which showed
only dimly as the shadows of night began to gather.
But even as she gazed at the darkened windows a light
sprang up in one of them.

The sight of it gave her a shock, causing her to catch
her breath, then she froze with fear as she realised that
the house was not empty. Could there be squatters or
burglars inside? No. They wouldn't switch on lights in
such blatant manner.

The thought gave her enough fragile courage to
leave the car and creep towards the window which she
knew allowed morning sun into the dining room. And
there a further shock awaited her.

A man sat at the paper-strewn table, watching the
screen of a word process. It took only a second for her
to recognise Guy Nelson.

The sight of him left her feeling dazed, but she
returned to the car and drove to the back of the house
where a glance showed the red Toyota parked in the
garage. Irritated, she fumbled for the back doorkey
given to her by Aunt Bea. It turned silently in the lock
and she was able to step into the kitchen. By that time
anger was really bubbling, and she swept into the dining

room to burst out wrathfully, 'What the devil are you doing here?'

Startled, Guy stared at her in disbelief. He stood up slowly before rasping in a hoarse voice, 'What the hell are *you* doing here?'

Linzi took a grip on her anger. 'I've come to do a painting of the cottage. It's at my aunt's request,' she informed him loftily. 'I'm afraid you'll have to go, and take whatever you're doing with you. There's definitely not room for us both in this place.'

His brows drew together as he gritted, 'Is that a fact? Then kindly understand that I'm not budging an inch. Richard gave me permission to come and work here, and here I intend to stay.'

'He had no right to do so,' Linzi blazed heatedly. 'This is my aunt's house—'

'Aren't you forgetting they're now married?' he drawled. 'If he can endow her with all his worldly goods, she can share hers with him. It's become a matter of what's yours is mine.'

'Has it, indeed?' She glared at him. 'And as Richard's nephew you imagine that gives you the right to break in, I suppose.'

'There was no need to break in,' he assured her calmly, having regained his composure before she had attained hers. 'Richard gave me his key.'

Her eyes widened. 'His—his key?'

'It's the one to the front door.' He took a Yale key from his pocket and laid it on the table.

Her face became flushed, her eyes remaining wide as she stared at it in silence.

He went on, 'You must have realised that Richard would have a key, considering the frequency with which he came to this place. I understand they've been lovers for years. . .or did you imagine they were too old for such frolics?' His tone had become ironical.

She avoided his penetrating gaze, which seemed to bore into her mind. 'I—I haven't given it much thought,' she prevaricated, still without looking at him.

No way would she admit that she'd guessed that his uncle and her aunt had been sleeping together. After all, whose business was it? Definitely not her own or Guy's. At last she added, 'In any case, *that* situation has no bearing on *this* situation.'

'What do you mean?'

'Well. . .naturally we can't stay in this house together. . .and. . .and alone.'

'Why not?' The query was snapped out.

'Because I don't intend to be compromised, old-fashioned as it may sound,' she informed him haughtily.

He laughed. 'Old-fashioned? It's positively medieval. Your mind must be back in the Dark Ages. Men and women are living together all over the world.' He looked at her in thoughtful silence for several moments, his eyes resting upon the mounds of her small breasts beneath the white blouse before moving to the shapeliness of her bare legs. At last he demanded quietly, 'Or is it just that you don't trust me?'

'I know what some men are like,' she mumbled, thinking of Garth Shaw, yet at the same time knowing she was behaving like an elderly, prudish spinster.

He scowled. 'Which means that you class me with them? Thank you very much.' The twist of his mouth betrayed anger, then he ground out, 'Lady, as far as I'm concerned you're as safe as a church. I wouldn't touch you with a forty-foot bargepole.'

She gasped at the insulting words, her chin rising as she stormed furiously, 'Thank heaven for that much. I couldn't bear you to touch me. . .' Then she swallowed back tears of rage.

A hand went to his forehead, as though he was suddenly horrified by what he had said, then he shook his head regretfully. 'I didn't mean that literally. I don't object to you personally—'

'No? You could've fooled me. You've been antagonistic right from the start—thanks to *Brenda*.' She took a deep breath then blazed at him, 'It's a pity you didn't marry *her*. You would have made a *charming* pair. . .absolutely *charming—*'

He cut in, almost shouting her down, 'Can't you understand that I'm trying to say I have a job to do? I don't want interruption, I don't want digression or—or interference that stops me from getting on with it.'

'Isn't *encumbrance* the word you're searching for?' she lashed back at him. 'Have no fear. . . I've no intention of being one.'

Guy made a visible effort to control himself. He stared at her in silence then spoke quietly. 'I'm trying to explain that I need solitude in which to work. Is it possible to get that point through to you?' he demanded grimly.

She stared at the word processor and at the papers littering the table, and although she told herself that she had no interest in what he was doing curiosity made her ask, 'What sort of work?'

'I'm writing a book. It's what I do.' The words came casually.

She refused to sound impressed. 'Sex-laden fiction, no doubt.'

His mouth tightened. 'Is that meant to be a sneer?'

She felt contrite. 'No. I really didn't mean. . .'

'You just thought that pornographic erotics would be the type of book I'd write. Well, you're wrong, because it's non-fiction. It's a book in the early gold-mining days of the Coromandel Peninsula. I presume you know there was gold in the area?'

'Of course I know,' she retorted scornfully. 'You must consider me to be thoroughly ignorant, or is that meant to be another insult?'

He shrugged, then explained, 'Not everyone is interested in the history of the district in which they live. Many are content to remain completely ignorant.'

Further curiosity forced her to ask, 'How far have you got with the project?'

He indicated the piles of papers. 'I've gathered a mount of material. It has to be sorted and put together, and for that I need space and a quiet place in which to work. . .*without interruption*.'

She felt slightly puzzled. 'Why not do it in Auckland? Isn't that where you live?'

'Yes. My other books have been written there, but I've lost my quiet flat at short notice through a fire that started in the flat next door.'

Linzi was unable to hide her surprise. 'Your other books? How many have you had published?'

'Oh. . .about eighteen over the last ten years.' He sent her a rueful glance. 'Obviously my name means nothing to you.'

She looked at him in silence, suddenly feeling completely idiotic. Guy Nelson. . . Of course. . . But she hadn't realised he was *that* Guy Nelson. Why hadn't Aunt Bea told her that Richard's nephew was an author whose non-fiction historical works were so well-known? But, now that she came to think of it, she'd seen very little of her aunt during the last year. Knowing Richard would probably be at Kauri Cottage, she hadn't wished to intrude.

Guy offered further explanation. 'After the fire I had to move into another flat on a temporary basis, but there were three other chaps in it and conditions were noisy and cramped. I was moaning about it to Richard when he suggested that I should come here to finish the book.'

'Without telling Aunt Bea about it,' Linzi said bleakly.

'I wouldn't know about that, but at least it's better for the cottage to be occupied, rather than standing empty and at the mercy of people who could break into it.'

'I suppose you're right,' she agreed with reluctance. No doubt Richard had been concerned about Bea's property, and as she thought of the tall, good-looking man whose dark hair was now grey at the temples she visualised the day when Guy would look just like him.

However, the fact that this man had got here first

was no reason for her to back down and creep away; therefore she came to a decision that made her say, 'Which room have you settled in?'

He sent her a wicked grin. 'The one Uncle Richard pretended to be sleeping in when he was here.'

She ignored the reference to her aunt's love affair. 'In that case I'll take Aunt Bea's room. And I'll use the third bedroom as a studio,' she added as an afterthought.

'Then you intend to stay?' The question came sharply.

'Yes. I'll keep away from you as much as possible. You'll not be disturbed by continuous chatter coming from me.'

'That'll be a relief.' He sent her another grin and then asked in a casual tone, 'Can you cook?'

'Of course I can cook.' She sent him a level glance. 'Although anyone who waits around for me to bang that dinner gong will find themselves becoming very hungry.'

His brows rose as he considered her thoughtfully. 'That's strange. You almost had me thinking you'd be different. . .but you're not.'

'Different?' The word needled her. 'Different in what way?'

'For one mad moment I thought you'd be kinder to a starving man, but obviously you're as hard as nails,' he informed her grimly.

The suggestion that he considered her to be that type of person held a sting which caused her to bristle with irritation. 'Why should I be kind to a man who wishes to see the back of me—a man who thinks only the worst of me? Besides, when you're ready for a meal I'll be painting out of doors. I'll have sandwiches with me.'

His words made her recall the sandwiches she had in the car. She hadn't eaten for hours, and now the thought of them made her feel hungry, so she said, 'If you'll excuse me I'll bring my things in.'

He made no reply, nor did he make any move to

help her, she noticed. Instead he sat down again and began to stare gloomily at the word-processor screen. It seemed to be proof of just how very unwelcome she was, but this did not surprise her because it was obvious that he had no wish for her to be there.

The task of collecting her belongings from the car did not take long, and as she carried them into the house the familiarity of the old place filled her with memories of childhood holidays with Aunt Bea. A warm glow of nostalgia helped to soothe her ruffled spirits and to lift the depression caused by that man in the dining room.

CHAPTER THREE

KAURI COTTAGE was an oblong building built in the simple style of many of the early homes. Near the front entrance the lounge and main bedroom lay on either side of the passage. Behind them lay the dining room, two smaller bedrooms and the bathroom, while the kitchen extended across the back of the house.

Apart from Aunt Bea's absence everything was the same, Linzi thought—except that she was not in the habit of sleeping in this front room, nor with a man occupying one of the other two bedrooms. Would he attempt to scare her from the place by making a sexual advance? The sudden fear made her turn to examine the doorlock, but there was no key.

She went out to the car again, this time to fetch her art materials which she put in the smaller of the remaining bedrooms. It was situated on the south side where the sun would not cause conflicting shadows on work resting on the easel. As she erected this folding equipment her nostrils were assailed by the tantalising aroma of fried onions. Guy, she realised, was cooking his own evening meal.

She continued to get the room organised, at the same time eating a sandwich which she felt would look meagre against whatever he was preparing for himself. Then, satisfied with what she was already considering to be her art room, she went to the front bedroom to unpack her suitcase.

In the midst of this task she was startled by the sound of the dinner gong which stood on the dining-room sideboard. 'Very funny, Mr Nelson,' she murmured to herself as its deep ring echoed through the house. 'I shall ignore it.' But the next instant she turned round to discover him standing in the doorway.

41

He took a rapid glance at her activities, then spoke quietly. 'Dinner is served.'

She looked at him blankly. 'Pardon. . .?'

'I said, Dinner is served. It's on the table so please don't allow it to go cold.'

Pride made her say, 'Thank you, but I've already had a sandwich.'

'Yes, I know. I saw you eating it with gusto. You can look upon it as a starter. Are you coming or do I throw it out? We eat in the kitchen,' he added drily.

She knew that to refuse would be not only ungracious but also stupid; therefore she said, 'I—I'm coming,' then followed him meekly to the kitchen table where he pulled out a chair for her to sit down.

As she did so she stared at the plate of steak, sautéed onions, mixed vegetables and French fried potatoes placed before her. 'I didn't expect this,' she murmured weakly, then felt humbled, and embarrassed to the point of being ashamed of her earlier attitude when he'd asked if she could cook.

He was an unusual man, she decided. Despite her refusal to cook for him, he had placed a meal before her. Why had he done this? Was it to make her feel small, or was he holding out a hand of friendship? OK, if he could hold out a hand, so could she, and suddenly she felt much warmer towards him.

The feeling she'd had when she'd first met him at the wedding—the desire to know him better despite the antagonism he'd shown—came surging back, making it easy to smile at him while steering the conversation towards his interests. And in listening to the problems of gathering historical information for his books she learnt a little more about the man himself, although she had no idea why it pleased her to do so.

He's a fanatic for accuracy, she realised. He strives to get at the truth of whatever he's writing about. It's what has made his books so successful. And suddenly she found herself looking at him with greater respect and a lot more interest.

Eventually she laid down her knife and fork. 'Thank you, that was delicious,' she said. 'The steak was so tender.'

He spoke casually. 'It was all out of the deep freeze, but, don't worry, your aunt's food will be replaced.' Frowning thoughtfully, he added, 'Bea knew she'd be leaving this place, so why did she leave the freezer bursting at the seams?'

'I suppose she expected me to be here.'

'Or did she expect us *both* to be here?' Guy queried musingly. 'Richard is sure to have discussed the idea of handing his key to me.'

She looked at him wide-eyed as a thought raced through her mind. 'I hope you're not suggesting what I fear you could be suggesting. . .'

'What might that be?'

'That—that my aunt set this up.'

'Isn't "matchmaking" the word you're seeking?' The question came drily as his mouth twisted.

She bristled at the irony of his tone, then spoke in defence of her aunt. 'No. Aunt Bea wouldn't try to organise my life. She knows I'm more than happy as I am.' She paused to stare at the table before adding, 'She also knows I'm anti-marriage at the moment. . . especially after a recent experience.'

'Is it a dark secret, or would you like to talk about it?'

She shied away from the thought. 'I've no intention of talking about it. I'd prefer to forget it.'

'It has put you off marriage?'

'Definitely.' Her lips closed in a firm line. To explain that Garth Shaw had shaken her faith in men would be a mistake, she decided. Guy would be sure that she was trying to exonerate herself. His desire to accuracy would demand more than her own explanation of the situation; nor was he likely to discard the picture already presented to him by Brenda.

Thinking about the situation, Linzi felt certain that Brenda's trouble was hurt pride. Brenda found it impossible to admit that Garth's interest had veered from herself to another woman. The other woman had stolen his interest, therefore it was all the other woman's fault. Or was it possible that Brenda was now taking a greater interest in this man who was so successful? Hadn't he said they'd had a boy-and-girl affair?

Irritated, she brushed the thoughts from her mind, then forced a smile as she said, 'I'll make coffee. Black or white?'

'Black, thank you. No sugar. Shall we have it on the front veranda? There's a full moon. It should be quite romantic.'

'Romance is the last thing I need at the moment,' she retorted more sharply than she intended. 'I'll thank you to remember it, no matter what ideas you imagine Aunt Bea might have had in mind.'

She left the table hastily, hoping he hadn't noticed the annoying flush that had crept into her cheeks. And as she attended to the coffee she began to suspect her aunt's motive for suggesting that the paintings of the cottage and the tree should be done during their honeymoon. Gradually, suspicion deepened into certainty.

It was easy to guess that Bea was floating on cloud nine, but was she so carried away by her own happiness that she wanted her niece to find similar joy with Richard's nephew? Sorry, Bea, Linzi thought with bitterness. If you'd known how low I am on Guy's popularity list, you wouldn't have even bothered to try. Then a sigh escaped her as she moved to lift the tray of coffee-cups and the home-made shortbread she had brought with her.

Guy took it from her, then strode along the passage towards the front veranda where there was a table and a small wooden settee suitable for two people. They sat on it, and she was immediately conscious of his thigh resting against her own. The touch was like an electric shock which made her vitally aware of how easily this man's aura seemed to find the power to reach out and envelop her.

Studiously, she stared ahead while sipping her coffee. As he had said, there was a full moon. It threw a brilliant pathway onto the sea, and because there was little or no wind the glowing sheen extended across the calm waters of the bay, turning it to silver. The gentle murmur of ripples breaking on the shore came to them, and above it rose the shrill, high-pitched chirping of cicadas gathered in nearby trees.

Linzi searched for a subject that would make her feel more normal, and, snatching at the long-winged insects, she remarked, 'The cicadas are noisy this evening—I suppose because it's warm.'

Guy spoke casually. 'That din comes from the males calling for mates. Didn't I say it was a night for romance?' The last words came teasingly.

She replied with studied sweetness, 'After courtship I presume the males will desert the females? No doubt even a cicada shakes off an emcumbrance.'

The moonlight showed a scowl on his face. 'Not all males are fickle. . .although of course there are numerous Garth Shaws in the world.'

This, she realised, was a jab at her, and although she felt the pain of it she did not allow it to show. Instead she smiled and said gently, 'You must be very fond of Brenda to be so concerned for her. Did you discover you were in love with her when it was too late?' Her voice had become sympathetic.

Hostility flared from him as he gave an evasive answer. 'I can't see how the state of my emotions can possibly interest you.'

Her tone was still gentle. 'Just call it sympathy for a man who intends to remain lonely because he can't have the woman he wants.'

'Well. . .it's something I have no intention of discussing.' Then his mouth twisted as he rasped, 'Nor do we need to discuss your own love life, because we know all about *that*, do we not?'

She replaced the coffee-cup on the saucer with a slight clatter. 'Heaven give me strength—' she began.

But he cut in, 'I've been waiting for you to deny the accusations Brenda has made. So far I've heard not one word,' he pointed out grimly as he turned to look at her. 'At least, none that convinces me,' he qualified.

'What use would it be when your mind is already made up?' she demanded wrathfully.

'None at all,' he admitted in a hard tone. 'So may we change the subject completely?'

'Delighted to do so,' she snapped, feeling an inner surge of frustration.

'OK.' He thought for a moment then queried, 'When do you intend to make a start on the art project?'

It took several moments to calm the anger bristling through her mind, but at last she took a deep breath that helped her to speak in a casual manner. 'Tomorrow morning I'll make a sketch of the cottage. By lunchtime it should have a layer of paint on the canvas. I'll be working with oils and will need to allow it to dry slightly before adding a further coat.'

'I can't imagine you just sitting waiting for it to dry.'

'Of course not. In the afternoon I'll take a fresh canvas and paint in a sky as background for the pohutukawa tree.'

He nibbled a finger of shortbread then said, 'In the morning I'll take a short time off to watch you work on the cottage.'

'*You will not*,' she protested sharply, the thought filling her with alarm. 'I do not like people breathing over my shoulder while I'm struggling to get the perspective of a building correct.'

'I see. Very well, I'll keep away.' He sounded offended.

She sensed his disappointment. It made her capitulate to the extent of saying, 'Well, perhaps you may watch, but not before I've got the cottage sketched to my satisfaction.'

He grinned. 'I understand. You don't want it to look as if it's lurching over in a drunken state.'

She laughed. 'Definitely not. Aunt Bea would be furious and my reputation as an artist would be ruined.' Then she went on more soberly, 'In any case, I also know you want to be alone in this place, so the sooner I finish these paintings, the sooner I'll be able to leave you to enjoy listening to the cicadas in solitude.'

'A most exciting prospect, I don't think!'

She snatched at his last words to exclaim vehemently, 'That's right—*you don't think*! Otherwise you'd realise how stupid it is to imagine I'm having an affair with Garth Shaw!' She paused to control the sudden anger that had risen within her, then said in a calmer voice, 'Sorry. I forgot that subject is supposed to be closed.' But she had said what he wanted to say and felt better for it.

Guy's eyes remained hooded for several long moments. He made no response to her small outburst, but eventually he broke the silence by reverting to the former topic. 'I presume there'll be no objection if I watch you paint the tree?'

'As long as there's no objection if I read your manuscript,' she returned, instinct warning that this was not something he would welcome.

He frowned. 'Well. . .actually. . . I'm not in the habit of allowing people to—'

'Nor am I in the habit of painting before an audience,' she cut in. Good grief, how could she do competent work with this devastating man watching every brush stroke? Already she was beginning to feel the pull of his charisma, but in no way would she allow herself to succumb to it—especially as he had such a poor opinion of her integrity. Thoughtlessly she said, 'I think it will be much safer if we keep to our own domains. Yours is the dining room, mine is outside or in the third bedroom.'

'Safer? What do you mean by safer?' He turned to look at her, the moonlight betraying a glitter of interest in his eyes.

She thought rapidly. 'I mean that if we stay apart it should minimise this constant antagonism that flows between us. Don't tell me you're unaware of it, because I'll not believe you.'

'You're sure that's what you meant?' he asked softly.

'Of course. What else could I have meant?' she challenged him with a hint of defiance, finding it impossible to explain that on this narrow settee the pressure of his thigh against her own was having an effect on her. It was sending tingles towards her spine and making her blood race through her veins.

He turned away again, remaining silent while watching the glow on the water through narrowed lids. When he spoke it was in a low, deep voice, almost as if to himself. 'Strangely, I thought you meant something entirely different.'

'Like what?' She held her breath. Had he guessed her thoughts?

'Nothing. It's not important. It was just a silly notion.'

She felt vaguely deflated. Obviously the pressure of her hip against his own affected him not at all. He gave no sign that it could cause a flare of emotion between them, but what else had she expected? Nothing... Nothing at all.

In an effort to shake off the erotic thoughts jumping about in her mind she stood up abruptly, saying with decision, 'The dishes are waiting to be put into the dishwasher. I'll do it while you go back to the dining room.'

He stretched himself, as though relieved to be given more room on the seat. 'I'm finished for the day and the dishes can wait. I thought a walk along the beach would be pleasant.'

For a moment she wondered if she'd heard correctly. He was actually asking *her* to walk along the beach in the moonlight? No doubt he expected her to jump for joy at the suggestion...and if so he'd be disappointed. Choosing her words carefully, she said, 'If you'll excuse me I'll do the dishes. The beach is a rather difficult place at night. This west coast of the peninsula is not all smooth sand. There are many rough, stony areas—'

'I know perfectly well what this area of the beach is like,' he grated irritably. 'I can also find my way between the rough and smooth places. However. . .suit yourself.' Then, despite his statement about work being finished for the day, he returned to the dining room, closing the door behind him.

He's annoyed, Linzi thought, carrying the tray to the kitchen, where she attended to the dishes. After that she went to the third bedroom and began to sort out what she would need in the morning. As she did so she considered from which angle she would paint the cottage, realising that the final work on it must be done in the afternoon when the sun showed the building and its shadows to advantage. Yes. . .the cottage was definitely an afternoon picture, although the sketch and first coat could be done in the morning.

Restlessly, she returned to the veranda and stood staring through the moonlight towards a shrub-sheltered area which might be a suitable place to set her easel. To make sure of this she left the veranda and crossed the drive towards it, then turned and gazed back at the cottage. Yes, it would do nicely.

Her thoughts then turned towards the pohutukawa tree, which she had already decided to paint from the veranda. She did not think there was a better place from which to do it, but to be sure she made her way to an area which would give her a different view. To reach it she had to cross the road and move carefully over ground that was rough with gravel and large stones, but despite her care a stone turned as she trod on it. . .and so did her ankle.

She gave a yelp of pain, then toppled over and sank to the hard boulders. Her leg stretched before her, she sat waiting for the agony to subside, but instead of doing so it became worse. She could feel her ankle becoming bound with a tightness while an excruciating pain crept up her leg. Tears sprang to her eyes, trickling down her cheeks while she cursed the stupidity that had brought her out into the night.

She knew she had to get home, but to do so would now prove to be a problem. Her foot was too painful to put to the ground, and if she tried to hop over this stony area she'd be in danger of turning her other ankle. There was only one way to get there. She'd have to crawl.

She had no idea how long she sat waiting for the pain to at least become less severe. The minutes passed, and to add to her misery a chilly breeze swept in from the sea, causing her to feel cold. She began to shiver as though gripped by an ague, and she knew she *must* make an effort. Besides. . .there was the tide. *How far did it come up?* Then, as panic began to rise, she heard Guy's voice.

He called to her from the roadway. 'Hi. What are you doing there? It's a daft place to sit in the moonlight.'

She looked over her shoulder to see him striding across the stones towards her. Waves of relief flooded through her, bringing a fresh gush of tears, but she sniffed rapidly, sweeping them away.

He squatted beside her, his tone harsh as he rasped, 'I had no idea you were so allergic to me.'

She was taken aback. 'Allergic? Wh-what do you mean?'

'I asked you to go for a walk, remember? But you refused. A short time later you sneak out and go alone.' He sounded aggrieved.

'I did *not* sneak out!' she exclaimed emphatically.

He ignored her denial. 'I didn't miss you until I realised the house had become very silent. And then I discovered it to be empty. I can only presume you wanted a walk. . .but not with me.'

She shook her head, feeling too distressed to argue. 'I didn't go for a walk. I went to find a suitable place from which to paint the cottage.'

'At this hour? You must be crazy.' He stared at her in disbelief.

'I suppose you can look upon it as a mad impulse that was meant to save time in the morning. I'm anxious to get these two paintings finished as soon as possible—'

'So that you can scamper back to Thames. . .and Mr Shaw?' His voice had become heavily sarcastic.

She drew a hissing breath. 'If you go on about him again I'll—I'll scream my head off.' The tears welled.

'Oh, yes?' He sounded sceptical. Then, regarding her more closely, he said, 'You're shivering. Why do you continue to sit out here? Are you waiting for the tide to come up?'

'Of course not. It's—it's because I can't stand up. I've hurt my ankle.' The admission came tremulously.

He moved his position to take a closer look at her leg, then uttered a mild oath as he exclaimed, 'Even in this dim light I can see it's coming up like a balloon! Why the hell didn't you mention it at once?' His tone was suddenly irate.

'I—I've been hoping the pain would go away so I could walk. . .'

He stood up abruptly and with one swift movement swept her up into his arms. 'It'll be much easier if you hang on with your arms round my neck,' he informed her crisply, his tone indicating that this was necessary, rather than something he desired.

Linzi clung to him, and as they crossed the stony area she recalled the last time he had carried her. Again she became aware that she appeared to be little more than a featherweight in his strong arms, and as they crossed the road and went along the drive she was also conscious of the pressure of his arms holding her against his breast.

'This is the second time I've carried you,' he remarked nonchalantly as they entered the kitchen, where he lowered her gently to the cushioned window-seat. 'Last time it was because of shoes. Now then, let's look at the damage.'

He pulled another chair forward, and as she rested her leg upon it they regarded the ankle ruefully, the size and redness of it causing him to say, 'You'll have to keep off it for a while.'

Linzi began to protest. 'I can't do that. I must get these paintings done. I want them finished and framed before Aunt Bea and Richard return. They're to be wedding presents.'

Guy continued to frown at the ankle. 'We'll see how it behaves. In the meantime we'll give it what assistance we can. I wonder if there's such a thing as a bandage in the house? At least I know there's ice.'

'Aunt Bea usually keeps a first-aid kit in the bathroom cupboard,' she informed him gloomily, beginning to feel depressed.

He disappeared, then returned with a box containing the necessary items. His capable, well-shaped hands bandaged her ankle firmly, and as he bent over the task a lock of dark hair flopped over his forehead.

Looking at it, Linzi was gripped by an intense desire to smooth it back, but of course that was unthinkable. Even so she had to clench her fists tightly to resist the temptation.

He looked up to meet her eyes. 'That's not too tight?'

'It's just nice and firm, thank you,' she said faintly, wondering why the impulse to touch him had been so strong.

'Good. Now we need a cold compress.' He went to the freezer and extracted the trays of small ice-cubes. They were tipped into a plastic bag which was carefully placed against the ankle bandage then wrapped in a towel to keep the ice pack in place. '"Rice" is the word,' he said enigmatically.

'*Rice. . .?*' Her eyes widened. 'I don't understand.'

He spelt the word 'R-I-C-E. When it comes to a sprain every junior nurse thinks of "rice". The letters stand for rest, ice, compression, and elevation, so you'll keep that leg up. And you'll take a couple of aspirins as well.'

'But. . . I haven't got a headache,' she protested.

'You've got an ache at the other end. The aspirins will help to lessen the pain. There are sure to be some in this first-aid kit.' He found them, then handed her two with a glass of water.

She washed them down, and as she returned the glass she spoke in a humble tone. 'Thank you for helping me—I feel so grateful.'

The broad shoulders lifted slightly. 'Think nothing of it.'

'But I do think something of it. You're very kind. . . especially to one you'd rather see a hundred miles away.'

He grinned. 'You can bring that down to ninety-five.'

'I can?' She felt surprised and pleased, her face brightening as she queried, 'What have I done to deserve that concession?'

He hesitated, then said, 'Let's just say you've brought a little stimulation into the place. To be honest, I was beginning to feel rather stale, and that state could become reflected in my writing.'

'But I thought solitude was your main objective.'

'Not to the point of it becoming a bore. One can have too much.'

'OK I'll also be honest. When I first arrived I felt annoyed to find you here. Now I'm only too thankful that you *are* here.' The admission came frankly, her eyes glowing with sincerity.

He nodded. 'So that makes us quits. And as we're stuck with each other we'd better make the best of it. I suggest that we call a halt to any further bickering. I'm a peaceful man at heart.'

She drew a long breath. 'Well, *that's* pretty rich. Right from our first meeting *you* have been the one who has shown antagonism to *me*.' Then she controlled the niggle of irritation as she went on, 'Actually, I'm also a peaceful person—apart from times when I'm *wrongly accused*. Then I'm inclined to lash out in all directions.'

However, she knew that she hadn't really lashed out, otherwise she would have tried to explain the problem of Garth Shaw in words that were loud and clear. And the reason she had not done so was that she wanted Guy to discover the truth of that situation for himself. She wanted him to learn that Brenda had lied about her having an affair with Garth. It had to be this way because he'd never believe anything she herself said about it.

The knowledge of this lack of faith in anything she had to say about the situation made her feel depressed. A wave of weariness engulfed her, causing her shoulders to droop and a yawn to escape her.

Guy regarded her closely. 'You've gone rather pale,' he said. 'You're probably feeling worn out. I'll carry you to the bathroom and then to bed.'

The suggestion jerked life into her, causing her cheeks to flame as she retorted sharply, 'No, thank you. The night a man carries me to bed has not yet arrived.'

He scowled at her with undisguised anger. 'I have no intention of *getting in* with you, so you can let your mind rest on that score.'

Her cheeks became an even deeper red as the snub registered. 'I *mean* I must be able to get there under my own steam.'

He continued to glower at her. 'That foot must be kept off the ground. You must not try to walk on it.' The words were gritted at her in a manner that suggested she was too dumb to understand that fact.

'But I must be able to get around without being carried,' she argued. 'If I can't get on with my paintings I'll go mad from sheer frustration. Can't you *see*?'

'I can see you're too stubborn for your own good.'

'Besides, as I said before, the sooner the cottage and tree are finished, the sooner I'll be out of your hair.'

'I'm almost beginning to wonder if my hair can do with a spot of ruffling. . .at least a little. . .'

She made no reply, mainly because she was unsure of his meaning. Surely he couldn't mean that he *wanted* her to prolong her stay...? And yet he'd said she had brought stimulation. Then, brushing the thought aside, her mind returned to the problem of her own mobility, and suddenly she knew what to do. The answer lay, or rather stood, in the broom cupboard.

Indicating the narrow door, she said, 'Would you please fetch the broom to me? And I'd also like that small handtowel hanging near the sink.'

He passed the requested items to her, then watched with an amused smile while she wrapped the towel round the head of the broom. It was held in place by safety pins from the first-aid kit, and then the padded head was fitted beneath her armpit.

She sent him a smile of triumph. 'You see? Now I have a crutch. I can walk without putting my foot to the ground.' She took a few hopping steps, using the broom for balance. They were slow and awkward, but at least she could move along.

'Very resourceful,' he muttered with a hint of admiration. 'I can see you're smart as well as stubborn. Now you can go to bed without my help.'

Had he sounded almost regretful? she wondered, making her way to the bathroom. Of course not.

A short time later she got into bed without too much trouble, although a restless night followed. It was caused by discomfort in her ankle, and by thoughts that persisted in veering towards Guy Nelson.

At times she could almost feel the arms that had carried her from the shore, and she could see his hard, lean body stooping before her while he attended to her ankle. She could also see the lock of dark hair that had fallen across his brow, but perhaps her most vivid vision was of the pentrating gaze from his hazel eyes. It was almost as though they continued with a relentless questioning about Garth—although she knew that this would be on behalf of Brenda—and at last she thumped the pillow from sheer frustration.

Linzi was not in the habit of experiencing this sort of impact from a man. Most of the men with whom she'd had contact had remained as casual friends, but instinct warned that Guy Nelson was different. He had rocked her senses with the force of an earthquake, and she knew that she was not one to be listed in the category of casual friends.

By the early hours of the morning she knew that she had to wash him from her mind, and she also knew that there was only one way to do that: she must complete the paintings she'd come to do, and then go home to Thames. He'd be most unlikely to have thoughts of continuing this friendship—if friendship it could be called—especially with Brenda on his mind, and despite his relationship to Richard she doubted that she'd see him again.

When morning came she felt bleary-eyed from lack of sleep. Her ankle was colourful, and although the swelling had subsided a little it was still painful. With the help of the broom she hopped to the bathroom where she washed with difficulty before getting dressed and making her way to the kitchen for breakfast.

When it was finished Guy regarded the ankle critically while reminding her that she must keep off it. 'You'd be wise to sit in the lounge and watch TV. . .so long as you don't allow the sound to blare through the wall,' he said in a voice that rang with command.

Her expression became defiant. 'I've no intention of doing that. I have my trusty crutch and I'll carry my things out one by one with my free hand.' She got up from the table, tucked the towel-wrapped broom-head under her arm, then made her way into the third bedroom where she bent to pick up her folded easel.

He followed her, at the same time declaring impatiently, 'OK, I'll help you.' Then he snatched at her wooden paint-box, her stool, and a canvas board. 'Now then, where do you wish to sit, Miss Determination?'

She hopped ahead of him slowly, leading the way to the position she had chosen the previous evening. It was a secluded corner on a neighbouring section of empty land, and, hidden by brushy manuka bushes, she knew she'd be able to work unobserved.

Guy opened the easel, placed it in a firm position, then saw her settled on a stool with the box of oils open beside her.

She looked up at him gratefully. 'Thank you, Guy. I'll be all right now, so please forget about me.'

He stared at her bleakly. 'I wish I could. . .but you worry me.'

'You mean you worry about how long I'll be here to interfere with your work?' The question came bitterly.

'It's not that exactly. Last night I lay in bed thinking about you—' He stopped abruptly, scowling, as though annoyed with himself for having made that admission.

She caught her breath. 'You *did*? Are you sure it was about *me*, rather than about somebody else?'

'Of course I'm sure. I'm not yet ready to enter a nuthouse for the confused. I'll see you at lunchtime. I'll make sandwiches.' He turned and strode away without a backward glance.

She sat watching him return to the cottage, his feet almost stamping as his long legs made short work of the distance between it and her shrub-sheltered corner. His words continued to spin in her mind, and the more she thought of them, the clearer their message became. She was 'an encumbrance' and a confounded nuisance.

The knowledge grated sufficiently to bring a sting of tears. She dabbed at them angrily with a rag not yet soiled by turpentine or oil paint, then she found a stick of charcoal and, beginning with the nearest gable, began to sketch the old cottage onto the canvas board.

Sketching, Linzi had long since learnt, required the type of concentration that wiped the mind clear of everything else. And now it acted as a therapy to push all thoughts of Guy Nelson into the background. . .at least until lunchtime, when a glance at her watch indicated that it was time to begin making her way back to the house.

She grabbed the broom, struggled to her feet, then stood back to view her efforts. The sketch was coming along nicely, and, feeling satisfied, she pushed everything beneath the concealing bushes before setting off towards the cottage.

When she reached the back doorsteps she found difficulty in getting up them, but she refused to call for help. Then, in the kitchen at last, she sank into a chair just as the ring of the phone in the front hall pealed through the house. She sat still, listening as Guy's crisp tones came to her ears.

'Hello? I don't recall telling you I'd be here... Oh, well, if you say so perhaps I did.' There was a silence while he listened for several long minutes, then he said, 'My dear, are you quite sure about that?'

Linzi caught her breath. *My dear?* Only a woman could be on the other end of the line. And that woman had to be Brenda, although why she felt so certain about this she had no idea. Then she froze as his next words hit her ears.

'I'm afraid I'm unable to do anything about it. At present I have my own problems.'

Linzi bit her lip, guessing that she was his 'problem', and for some strange reason the thought wrapped her in a shroud of depression.

Guy's voice continued with a hint of command. 'You must talk to Garth. Try to forgive and forget. Try to be a little kinder to him. It shouldn't be too difficult.'

Garth. The name sharpened Linzi's senses. So she had been right. Brenda *was* on the line. No doubt she'd found an excuse to phone Guy. Even if only to talk to him and to hear his voice. Yet instinct warned there was more to it than that.

She thanked heaven that it couldn't possibly concern herself. At least, she was unable to see how it could. Or was she wrong about that?

CHAPTER FOUR

LINZI had no wish to hear more of the telephone conversation; therefore she went to the bathroom, closed the door and washed her hands. When she returned to the kitchen Guy had taken two plates of sandwiches from the fridge and was pouring coffee.

There were grim lines about his mouth, and she guessed that he was in a disgruntled mood. Making an effort to alleviate it, she forced cheerfulness into her voice as she said, 'Thank you for the sandwiches. Ham and crushed pineapple. . .cheese and tomato. . .they're very tasty. This evening I'll prepare our dinner.'

He ignored the statement and rasped a question at her. 'When did you last see Shaw?'

She paused with a sandwich halfway to her mouth, staring at him wide-eyed. 'Garth? It was on the path after the wedding reception. You were with me at the time. Why do you ask?' she queried, feeling sure that his question had something to do with the phone call.

The hazel eyes narrowed, watching her intently, then his voice became deceptively soft. 'Are you sure that was the last time you saw him?'

'Of course I'm sure,' she snapped. 'What is this? Has somebody accused us of being together?'

'You could say so,' he drawled.

'Then whoever said so was lying,' she declared vehemently.

He rasped another question at her. 'How did you fill in your time between the wedding and coming here? Or do you intend to tell me to mind my own damned business?'

'Not at all,' she said, keeping a grip on her steadily rising temper. 'I spent most of the time in my studio completing orders that were waiting to be framed.

After that I collected the necessary art materials to bring here.'

'Shaw didn't help you with those framing jobs by any chance?' The words came silkily.

The suggestion amazed her. 'That's a daft idea. We're in opposition in business—or have you forgotten that small fact?'

He helped himself to another sandwich as he said, 'It's been suggested that your so-called opposition is little more than a blind.'

'Suggested by whom?' she demanded indignantly. 'Brenda, no doubt.'

'I have not said so.' He was watching her closely.

'You don't have to,' she flushed at him angrily. 'But it's obvious you believe that to be the situation. Well, let me tell you you're dead wrong. And if that's what Brenda believes she must be out of her tiny mind, unless. . .' She fell silent as a thought struck her.

'Yes? Unless what?' he demanded sharply.

'Unless she's using the idea to further a plan,' she declared as the thought became even more solidly fixed in her mind.

'I don't understand. What plan could she possibly have?' The question came in a dangerously quiet tone that warned her to think twice about her reply.

She hesitated, but went on regardless of the anger that might arise. 'To be honest, I think she's disillusioned with her marriage to Garth and I can't say I blame her.'

His eyes became piercing. 'You mean she wants it to end?'

'Yes. But then other troubles would begin. If she left him she would need someone to take care of her. Brenda is not a career woman, nor are jobs thick on the ground for one who hasn't been in the workforce for years,' Linzi said thoughtfully.

'So what do you think she has in mind? What's this plan you're hinting at? I'm still in the dark about it.'

Again she hesitated, knowing that she was risking his

wrath by uttering criticism of one who had been his friend for so long and for whom he seemed to hold a definite fondness. However, she had gone too far to draw back; therefore she said, 'I can't help wondering if she intends to use an imaginary affair between Garth and myself as an excuse for leaving him.'

'In that case you must fear she has evidence to enable her to do so.' His voice held accusation. 'Nor do I think she would go running home to her parents. They're very strong on the sanctity of marriage.'

Linzi smiled. 'No, she wouldn't head in their direction.'

'Then where. . .?' He fell silent as her meaning dawned upon him.

'She'd fly to you, of course. The proverbial homing pigeon,' Linzi said frankly, determined to make sure that her suspicions registered with him, yet not wishing to sound too dogmatic about them.

He stood up abruptly, leaving the table to pace about the room while he thought about it, until suddenly he paused to swing round and face her. His expression glacial, he rasped, 'Before I can believe she'd leave him, I must know the extent of his affair with you. How and when did you first become involved with Shaw?'

Her face pale, she took a deep breath to control her anger. At the same time she realised that now was the moment to reveal the harassment she had been forced to endure from Garth. 'Sit down and finish your sandwiches,' she said wearily. 'I'll tell you all about it.'

'Start with when you first met him,' he ordered in a tone that indicated he meant to draw forth every detail.

She looked at him in silence, trying to collect her thoughts. Already she was regretting her last words. Tell him about the irritations she'd endured from Garth Shaw? Give him details of how Garth had tried to seduce her? She'd be a fool to do so.

Looking at his handsome face, she found herself wishing she *could* tell him. It would be a relief to unburden herself of those memories—if only she could rely on him lending a sympathetic ear. But his granite expression warned that he'd never believe her. He would think she was lying in an effort to cover her own indiscretions.

'Well?' he prodded. 'How and when did you become involved with Shaw?'

The question jolted angry words from her. 'I have never been *involved* with him—at least, not in the way you mean. Nor has there ever been an *affair* of the sort you suggest.'

'But you did go to work for him. I wonder why?' he murmured.

His tone caused further annoyance that made her reticent. There was no need to explain that while working in her father's accountancy office she had seen Garth's advertisement for an assistant and the opportunity to learn to frame her own paintings had been too great to resist so she had applied for the job.

Her silence made him say, 'You're not telling me very much.'

She shrugged. 'There's little to tell. He advertised for someone to learn the trade. I got the job.'

'I'm not surprised. You really are a woman to catch the eye.' His eyes followed the clean line of her jaw and the smoothness of her throat.

His scrutiny brought colour to her cheeks, especially as, too late, she recalled that while outside she had undone the top buttons of her blouse. Startled, she guessed that the low V of the neckline was now offering him more than a hint of cleavage, and her colour deepened as his eyes went from it to the small mounds of her breasts. 'It was very warm outside,' she muttered, making haste to fasten the buttons.

'And at times mighty warm in the back room of the shop, I'll be bound,' he gritted savagely. 'It's a wonder there was any framing work done at all.'

Furiously, she thumped her empty coffee-mug down on the table, then raged from between clenched teeth, 'I can see it's useless talking to you. Your mind is well and truly made up regarding the relationship between Garth and me.'

His jaw tightened. 'Can't you understand that it's the thought of you and Shaw in the back room that makes me see red?'

The memory of Garth and herself in the back room also made Linzi see red, but she forced herself to become calm as she said, 'No doubt you see red on behalf of Brenda—a whole wall of fire, in fact. Oh, yes. . . I understand perfectly.'

His eyes glittered with anger. 'I very much doubt that you do, but please go on. You said you'd tell me about it, remember? So what *did* happen in the back room?'

She looked at him steadily. 'I learnt to frame pictures, of course. I learnt to measure the mouldings correctly and to cut perfect corners. I also learnt to cut mounts for watercolours and to cut glass without cutting my fingers. Garth noticed I was very good at it, and after a short time—' She stopped, biting her lip and feeling annoyed by her runaway tongue.

Her altered expression was not lost on Guy. 'Go on. What happened after a short time?' he demanded, his gaze searching her face.

Linzi felt trapped. She knew that she had to tell him something, so decided to enlighten him with the truth. 'It wasn't long before Garth began dropping hints about a partnership,' she admitted.

'You mean a business partnership?' Guy queried, his eyes now narrowing thoughtfully.

She shook her head dolefully. 'At first I thought so, but when he began to make passes at me I realised he meant a different sort of partnership.' She stopped, looking at him doubtfully. 'Guy, I can't believe you really want to hear about this.'

'Try me. I'll tell you when I'm bored,' he snarled.

'Well. . .over and over again I heard all about Brenda's constant nagging and how she didn't understand him—'

Guy snorted. 'The poor fellow. That's real sad.'

'And then he reached the stage of being unable to keep his hands off me.' The admission came despite herself.

'And so you had sex.' The words were lashed at her with the coldness of ice.

'*No, we did not.*' Her face turned scarlet as she almost screamed the denial. 'How *dare* you suggest it?'

'OK, OK, simmer down. I merely wondered. Lots of people have sex, in case you're unaware of the fact.'

'Not with me, they don't,' she spat, her face still flaming as her fury loosened her tongue still further. 'I'll tell you this—on the last occasion he tried to force me.'

Guy drew a sharp breath. 'Are you sure he actually meant to—?'

'Of course I'm sure. Don't you think I knew what he had in mind? I had to struggle and fight like a maniac. Fortunately the bell in the front shop rang. I threatened to scream and he let me go. I got the hell out of the place and never went back.'

Guy's face was grave as he stared at her in silence until he said in a sympathetic tone, 'You poor girl. I'll bet you raced home to your mother.'

'I did not. I raced like mad to my father, who was still in his office. He was infuriated. It was all I could do to prevent him from going to Garth...but the thought of returning gave me a fit of the horrors. We didn't go home to Mother until we'd both calmed down, and that took quite a time. That evening he suggested that I should start in business on my own.'

Guy looked at her grimly as he said, 'It's a long way from the story Brenda told me.'

She glared at him, her expression bleak. 'I'll bet it is. But that's *my* story and I'm sticking to it. You may believe it or not as you choose. Now, if you'll excuse me, I'll go back to my work.'

'Wait. There's something else I'd like to know. Why has it taken you so long to tell me about this?'

She gazed at him unflinchingly, her blue-green eyes shadowed by their dark lashes. 'I wouldn't have told you now if you hadn't brought up the subject. You asked when I'd last seen Garth, remember?'

Morosely, he stared at the table. 'That's right, I did.'

'After that one thing led to another with you dragging it from me.'

'I still think you could've told me about it earlier. Why on earth couldn't you have?' He sounded exasperated.

'You can call it pride. You were so sure I was having an affair with Garth. Perhaps you still are. Maybe you think I've told you a pack of lies.'

'Then hear this: if there's one thing I loathe, it's to be told lies.' His face hardened as he glared at her. 'When I know a person has lied to me I never believe another word that person says.'

'Then the next time you see Brenda try shaking the truth out of her,' Linzi flung at him, then paused as a thought crossed her mind. 'Or perhaps it would be better to shake the truth out of Garth, if that's possible. After all, Brenda will know only what Garth has told her.'

His face cleared, the pained expression changing to one of relief. 'Of course...it all rests upon what that rat has told her. I feel sure she would never knowingly lie to me.'

'Wouldn't she? That's what *you* think,' Linzi retorted, making no effort to keep the irony from her voice. 'I must say such faith is quite touching.' Then, irritated because she was not at all sure that Guy believed her story, she bent and grabbed the broom, which was lying on the floor near her chair. Struggling to her feet, she leaned against the table, shoved the head beneath her armpit, and hopped from the room without a backward glance.

As she moved slowly back to where her painting equipment lay she told herself that she was being a fool for allowing the issue to upset her. It didn't matter what *that man* believed or disbelieved about her. Yet deep down she knew that it *did* matter, and by the time she put a brush to the canvas she was seething with vexation.

But, as usual, the concentration necessary for painting soothed her nerves, and a short time later, when working steadily, she became aware of Guy striding towards her. The sight of him made her heart beat more rapidly, and again she felt pain from the knowledge that he'd been so sure that she was having an affair with his friend's husband. *Had* been sure. . .or was *still* sure? she wondered dismally.

When he reached her side he stood motionless, regarding her work. 'It's coming along nicely,' he approved. 'I'm glad you haven't made the cottage too large. It has enabled you to get the distant hillside and trees into the background.'

His words pleased her, causing her to smile as she pointed out, 'If I'd made it larger I'd have lost the feel of it being a cottage.' Then she sat back, pretending to rest, but in reality afraid that her hand might shake if she continued to paint while he watched. It would tell him that he was having an effect on her, and that was something she wished to avoid at all costs.

He said, 'I thought you intended making a start on the pohutukawa trees during the afternoon.'

She hesitated, then admitted, 'I changed my mind. It would have been such an effort to carry everything to a new place.'

'Your pride at work again? It wouldn't allow you to ask for my help? Really, I could shake you,' he said impatiently.

'Could you indeed?' She sent him a level glance. 'Where did I get the impression that you have no wish for interruption to your work? I also recall the word "encumbrance" being mentioned.'

He frowned. 'I seem to have given you the idea that this book is sacrosanct.'

'Well, isn't it?' She sent him a look of pure innocence.

'It's not so sacred that I can't drag myself away to lend a helping hand,' he growled. 'Or do you see me as somebody who is completely immersed in his own interests?'

'No...of course not,' she faltered, shifting uncomfortably on her stool. How *did* she see him? She feared to ask herself.

He noticed the movement. 'Is your ankle worrying you?'

'It aches,' she admitted, not wishing to reveal just how much.

'That's not surprising. You are supposed to be keeping it raised, preferably with an ice-pack attached to it.' He stared at her ankle, then whipped the canvas board from the easel.

'What are you doing?' she protested.

'I'm folding your easel.' He grinned, loosening the screws. 'You've done enough painting for today. I'm taking you over the hill to town, so you can close your paint-box.'

'You're being very high-handed,' she declared indignantly, feeling that she should put on a show of some sort, rather than go like a mouse.

'I'm the overbearing, bossy type—in case you haven't noticed.'

'Oh, yes, I've noticed, although I'd have used the word "dominant" rather than "overbearing".' Or perhaps 'masterful', she thought privately.

'Thank you for the distinction,' he murmured, his sensuous mouth curving into a faint smile as he watched her wipe her brushes before closing the box that held numerous tubes of oil paints. Then, when the task was complete, his hands went to her arms, helping her up from the stool. But instead of releasing her he drew her closer, then bent swiftly and kissed her lips.

Brief as the moment was, the pressure of his mouth on her own sent sparks of electricity dancing through

Linzi's blood. She caught her breath then gaped at him. 'What was that for?' she demanded in a voice that was not quite steady.

'Appreciation of the kind word. All men like to be thought dominant, although I'm not as dominant as you imagine.'

She gazed at him dumbly, still feeling shaken by the inner turmoil that his kiss had caused. Oh, yes, you are, she decided. It's just that you don't flaunt it. And, what's more, you're *more* than dominant. You're also kind and you have integrity. But instead of voicing the thoughts jumping about in her mind she merely asked, 'Why are we going to town?'

'For milk and fresh vegetables,' he informed her. 'Items to replace everything we've used from the freezer. And I need a photo of the plaque on Ring's Bridge. You've seen it, of course.'

She nodded, still obsessed with the thought of his kiss, yet doing her utmost to forget it. 'Aunt Bea showed it to me years ago, but I can't recall the exact wording or much about the man.'

He handed her the broom with a slight bow, then said with mock formality, 'Allow me to enlighten you, because without Charles Ring I wouldn't be writing this particular book. He is famous for being the first man to discover gold in New Zealand.'

'That's right. It was in 1852. . .but that's all I know.' Why had he kissed her? The question continued to buzz in her brain.

As they made slow progress towards the cottage Guy told her about Charles Ring's determined searching along the creek beds for gold. But suddenly he broke off to say, 'Are you sure you're interested in all this?'

'Of course I'm interested,' she assured him hastily. 'How could I be otherwise—?' She stopped abruptly, knowing that anything that interested this man was also of vital interest to herself. However, it was not possible to say so; therefore she went on dreamily, 'It's difficult to believe that sleepy Coromandel was where the New Zealand gold-rushes began.'

'I don't find it difficult,' Guy said. 'The town still retains a Victorian character. Some of the buildings could be out of a Wild West film. It's one of the reasons I grasped the opportunity to work here, especially as the cottage was built not so very long after those days. It has an atmosphere of its own.'

'You mean it *did* have an atmosphere before I arrived to shatter the pure air with the odour of turpentine and linseed oil...and to make a pest of myself with a sprained ankle,' she said, feeling suddenly guilty for having intruded into his chosen working area. But, after all, she hadn't *known* he'd be there, and there was Aunt Bea's request to be considered.

He sent her a tolerant smile. 'Don't worry too much about it. I have a feeling that tranquillity and serenity are just round the corner.'

'They are?' Her eyes were wide with questions. 'What makes you so sure? It sounds as if you think I'll be leaving quite soon.'

His shoulders lifted in a vague shrug while his eyes became hooded. 'It's just an idea that came into my head. You'll learn soon enough.'

She stared at him suspiciously, her thoughts darting back to the kiss he'd planted on her mouth for no apparent reason. Or had there been a reason? Had he meant to convey that more would be expected of her if she remained under this same roof?

Her suspicions continued to simmer while she prepared to go to town. She removed the ankle bandage, then showered, sitting on a stool, at the same time washing her hair.

Strangely, the soothing waters seemed to wash away her misgivings about the man, and she began to tell herself that she was being a fool. Guy was not another Garth Shaw. He would never make advances that would send her rushing from the cottage—not that she *could* rush at present—and with this comforting thought she later took extra care with her make-up.

He worked in the dining room while waiting for her, and when she appeared in the doorway he stopped sorting papers, then stood up to regard her in silence. His eyes became alight with undisguised approval as they swept over the yellow and white summer dress before coming to rest on the auburn hair curling about her shoulders. 'You look as fresh as the proverbial daisy,' he said in a low voice.

'Thank you.' She sensed his sincerity and felt pleased.

His lips twitched. 'It's a pity the broom ruins the picture. Do you intend hobbling round town with it? You'll cause a sensation.'

She knew the broom must look ludicrous, and tried not to feel hurt by his amusement. 'I shall sit in the car while you do the shopping. In any case it is beginning to make my arm feel sore.'

'Then drop it at once.'

'I can't. I need it to get to the car.' She turned and began to make her way towards the back door. By the time she reached it he was at her side. The broom was taken from her and she was swept up into his arms. Her body, treacherous as ever, thrilled to his touch while the blood rushed to her face.

'This is becoming a habit.' He grinned, staring down into her eyes.

Their gazes held for several long moments before her lashes fluttered down to form two dark crescents against her cheeks, then he carried her out to the car, even supporting her while opening the door to enable her to slide onto the seat. He really is kind, she thought.

The drive over the hill to the town was taken in silence until Linzi realised that Guy had turned along a side-road leading away from the shops. She sent him an enquiring glance and asked, 'Where are we going?'

'There's a convalescent home along this road.' The reply came nonchalantly, and moments later he turned into a driveway leading to the front door of a rambling house.

She turned to stare at him, suddenly alarmed by thoughts that leapt into her mind. Was this what he'd meant by serenity and tranquillity returning to the cottage? Did he intend to make arrangements for her to stay in this convalescent home? If so he'd have to think again because no way could he force her to stay here.

Agitatedly, she began to protest, 'Guy, I don't need—'

'I know exactly what you need.' The retort came crisply as he left the car and went up the steps to the veranda. He pressed the doorbell, and within moments a plump, smiling woman appeared. He followed her inside the house.

Linzi sat and fumed. How *dared* he imagine he could install her in this place because of a mere sprained ankle? OK, so perhaps she was becoming a pest and an—an *encumbrance*, but that didn't warrant his taking such measures to be rid of her. Tears of frustration welled into her eyes. She dabbed at them, then sat with closed lids while waiting for Guy's return.

A few minutes later she heard his voice coming from the veranda. Her eyes flew open, then her jaw sagged slightly at the sight of the objects in his hands. He was carrying a pair of light metal crutches that could be adjusted to her height. A wave of relief swept through her as she got out of the car eagerly, then stood on one foot while they were measured against her. 'Proper crutches!' she exclaimed.

'Very observant,' he commented drily. 'Didn't I say I knew what you needed? I've hired them for the duration.'

'Thank you. . .oh, thank you, Guy,' she said humbly, feeling mortified by the memory of her previous thoughts. How could she have so *stupidly* imagined that he intended her to stay in that place? Then she added, 'You really are very kind.'

Thinking about it, she decided that depression had been the cause of these negative thoughts. Lack of sleep through discomfort with her ankle, and the immobility the sprain had caused, had dragged her down. And with it had been the knowledge that Guy resented her presence. It had all combined to form an oppressive black cloud above her head. But he had done this for her, and suddenly the cloud lifted and floated away.

By the time they reached Ring's Bridge her depression had vanished. She got out of the car, eager to experiment with the crutches, then swung between them as they went towards the creek crossing.

Guy watched her action, an amused glint in his eyes. 'I trust they're an improvement on the broom?' he queried.

'Are they ever! Thank you again, Guy... I feel so grateful.' Her depth of feeling made her voice quiver.

He photographed the plaque which stated, 'THE FIRST GOLD FOUND IN N.Z. WAS DISCOVERED IN THIS AREA BY MR CHARLES RING IN 1852.' Then, tucking the camera back into its case, he said, 'I've read that the stream is known as Driving Creek because it was the driving force for a nearby sawmill. I presume it drove the wheel which set the rest of the works in motion.'

Linzi fell in with his mood. 'I suppose most things are driven by a power of some sort. Even people are driven by different urges.'

'You're right,' he agreed in a voice that had suddenly become grim. 'Nor is it difficult to guess at the urges that drove Shaw when he had you close at hand.'

She flushed. 'Why bring him up?'

'Because he persists in sitting at the back of my mind. He gnaws like the rat that he is. What do women see in such a man?'

'I don't know. You'll have to ask Brenda. She evidently sees something in him,' Linzi said, then immediately regretted the words, which she feared could arouse his anger even further because, of course, he was jealous. *That* was what gnawed at *his* mind. *Jealousy*. She felt sure of it. And his next words seemed to confirm that suspicion.

Glowering as he stared down into the creek, he said, 'I always imagined Brenda to be a sensible girl, yet she married *Shaw*.'

Linzi sought for words that would comfort him, but was unable to find anything suitable to say, until at last she muttered in a small voice, 'They say that love makes fools of many people.'

'Do they indeed?' he snarled. 'And who, may I ask, are "they"?'

'I understand that "they" are people in general.'

'Well, you may tell *them* that love will not be making a fool out of *me*,' he declared vehemently.

'That remains to be seen,' she retorted, then rushed on, 'And what's more I can guess why you were so eager to believe I was having an affair with Garth Shaw.' The last words were flung at him.

His expression became inscrutable. 'Why would I *want* to do that?'

She knew that she was treading on dangerous ground, but her suspicions came tumbling heedlessly. 'Because it would give you an excuse to comfort Brenda. No doubt you'd like me out of the house so that you could bring her here to do just that.' These facts became clearer to her as she spoke, and again she rushed on, 'This seems to be a case of the pot calling the kettle black. It turns you into a hypocrite, Guy Nelson.' She fell silent as the thoughts swirled about in her mind.

He stared at her bleakly, a muscle working at the top of his jaw as his voice became dangerously quiet. 'Go on. Is there more? So I'm a hypocrite?'

'Of course you are.' She spat the words. 'You *dare* to censure what you imagine is between Garth and me, yet you're itching to take his wife into your arms. If that's not hypocrisy, then you tell me what is.'

He began to laugh, as though seeing humour in her

words. 'Well, aren't you a contradiction? A short time ago you were telling me I'm kind, now you're spitting tacks at me. It must be the red in your hair.'

'It's not red,' she snapped furiously. 'It's *auburn*.'

'Maybe, but the sun is putting a few flames into it. They must be seeping through your entire body,' he said mockingly.

'It's not the sun, it's *you*,' she flared at him. 'You made me *mad* when you persisted with that *ridiculous* idea about Garth and me.' Frustration made her voice tremble.

He came closer, staring down into her face, his penetrating gaze raking her features. When he spoke his low voice held a strange huskiness. 'You should get mad more often. The red in your cheeks sends a diamond sparkle into those blue-green eyes. Have I told you that you're really quite lovely to look at?'

His last words acted as a soothing balm to take the heat from her anger. Her pulses quickened, and as his head bent a little lower a wild expectancy shot into her mind. He's going to kiss me, she thought. In spite of those awful things I've been saying, he's going to kiss me. It'll be the second time. . .

But he did not. For some reason he hesitated, and instead of laying his lips on her own he raised his hand to stroke her cheek with the backs of his fingers. Then he opened the car door for her.

His touch made her feel tense, while his words deepened the glow in her cheeks. Did he really think her face was easy on the eye? Was it possible that he didn't resent her presence in the cottage as much as she had imagined? Or would he gladly swap her presence for Brenda's? Yes, of course he would.

The thought of Guy holding Brenda against his heart was enough to send jabs of jealousy streaking through Linzi. She shook herself mentally, then listened to the warning that flashed into her mind. Just watch yourself with this charmer. You're becoming too attracted to him. . .and you don't mean a thing to him. His thoughts are wrapped up in Brenda, even if she is out of reach.

Or was she out of reach? Brenda had only to come to the end of her endurance of Garth's activities and file for divorce on the grounds of faithlessness and incompatibility. She could then fly straight to Guy who would no doubt be waiting for her with open arms. The thought caused a sharp breath to escape her while a pained expression settled upon her face.

A hint of her inner distress conveyed itself to Guy. He shot a rapid glance at her face then demanded abruptly, 'What's the matter? Does your ankle worry you?'

'I know it's there,' she admitted.

'But it was not the cause of that deep sigh,' he declared with perception. 'Come on, out with it. Tell me what's bugging you.'

She wrestled with the thoughts that again crowded into her mind, then found herself confessing, 'Actually, I was thinking about Brenda.' And then more inner turmoil forced her to pursue recklessly, 'She phoned you, didn't she?'

'Yes.' The word was snapped tersely.

She waited, hoping for further information, but his stony silence indicated that it would not be given to her. It is not your business, she reminded herself despite feeling hurt. At last, unable to bear his lack of communication on this subject that had suddenly become vitally important to her, she persisted with another question. 'Do you think Brenda has thoughts of filing for divorce?'

He grinned. 'With yourself as co-respondent?'

'*Me?*' The word jerked out as a squeak. 'She'd have difficulty in citing me as a co-respondent.' The mere thought made her cringe.

'Are you sure it would be so impossible? It would depend upon what Garth admitted concerning the matter. If he declared he'd been to bed with you it could be a matter of your word against his. After all, the opportunity has been there. Your parents are in Australia and you have the house to yourself.'

His words sent a chill sweeping through her. This was something her thoughts had not caught up with, but now that the possibility of such a ghastly situation lay before her she viewed it with dismay. Her parents would be sent into a state of shock; people would send sidelong glances at her and her business would suffer. It was all so sickening that she hardly knew the car had stopped outside the supermarket.

Guy twisted in his seat to stare at her. 'You're looking worried. Are you wondering what to wear to court for the hearing?'

'*No, I am not,*' she gritted from between clenched teeth.

'I'd suggest something demure and mouse-like. Something to make the judge think you're an innocent victim who is being tossed between a wolf and a vindictive wife. . .except that I'm not sure that Brenda is vindictive. Perhaps "injured" is a better word.'

His words did nothing to lift Linzi's spirits. 'I don't think you're taking this seriously,' she complained in an aggrieved voice.

'Should I be doing so?' he asked in a weary tone that hinted at boredom. 'Aren't you forgetting I have other things on my mind such as a manuscript to finish? Would it surprise you to learn that it must take precedence over arguments that spring up between you and Brenda?'

She sent him a cool stare. 'You surprise me. I've been given to understand that her welfare is your first priority.'

'Now you're being ridiculous,' he snapped impatiently. 'I'll admit I don't like to see her unhappy, but Brenda and I took separate paths long ago. She should be Shaw's first priority. . .but unfortunately his interests appear to have been diverted.'

His meaning hit her with force, causing her to draw a long, deep breath before speaking in a voice that was unsteady. 'I'll have you know I've *never* done a single thing to encourage him.'

'No?' He swept her with a swift glance of appraisal. 'But then you wouldn't have to. You've only to look in the mirror to see why he'd come loping along like a buck rabbit.'

She knew the words were meant as a compliment, but they gave her no pleasure. Instead they made her realise that he was a complex man who said nice things one minute, then moments later ruined them by uttering negative comments. 'You puzzle me, Guy—' she began.

'I do?' he cut in. 'That's because you're feeling tired. You'll sit in the car while I do the shopping, then we'll go home and you'll put your foot up with an ice-pack. By that time the sun will be over the yard-arm. I'll pour you a long, cool drink.'

She watched him stride into the supermarket. He was being nice to her again, she thought. Yes, he was being nice to her despite the fact that he itched to see the back of her—and despite the shadow of doubt hovering in his mind.

CHAPTER FIVE

EARLY evening was upon them before Linzi sat with her legs stretched along the length of the lounge settee while Guy squatted on a low stool beside her. He had placed cushions at her back, and now his strong, well-shaped hands were firm but gentle as they rolled the bandage round her ankle.

'How does it feel?' he queried, adjusting the ice-pack and securing it in position with a small towel.

'Much better now that my foot is not hanging down,' she admitted, then added gratefully, 'Thank you, Guy. You're very kind, but I've told you that before.'

'Think nothing of it.' His tone was dismissive. 'Now I'll get that promised drink.' He heaved his long form from the stool and left the room.

It was nice to be taken care of, she thought wistfully, gazing through the window. And then her attention was caught by the brilliant colours in the western sky where the varied hues of pink, mauve, red and yellow vied with each other to paint the clouds. The beauty of it stirred her own appreciation of colour, and when Guy returned to the room she exclaimed ecstatically, 'That's not sea out there, it's a mass of rippling gold!'

He paused to stare through the window then commented, 'Life's like that sunset—colourful one moment, dull the next.'

'I suppose you're right,' she sighed. 'Even now it's beginning to fade.'

'One must learn that nothing stays the same. Drink this—you need a pick-me-up.' He handed her a large crystal glass with ice and a slice of lemon floating on top of its clear, brimming contents.

She looked at it doubtfully. 'Is it gin and tonic? I hope the gin isn't too strong. I take very little alcohol.'

'A little of what you fancy does you good,' he said. 'This will wash your depression away.'

'Who says I'm depressed?' she demanded with a touch of defiance.

'I do. It's written all over you.' He scrutinised her face then added flippantly, 'It's probably all that worry about not knowing what to wear to court.'

She knew he was joking, but the words held a sting. In some intangible way they seemed to confirm that, deep down, he was not entirely sure that she was innocent where Garth Shaw was concerned. And, further, that he needed to have only a little patience before she gave her guilt away. His distrust, disguised by a veneer of kindness that was meant to lower her guard, upset her to the extent of causing her hand to shake.

He noticed it, then ordered, 'Drink your gin and tonic before you spill it. Then you might tell me what the hell's bugging you. Don't try to deny it, because I know something is gnawing at you.'

His abruptness caused her to pull herself together. She took several sips then said, 'What makes you so sure something's bugging me? You know nothing about me or my thoughts.'

'If it comes to that, you know nothing about me — not that you'd have any desire to do so, of course,' he commented drily.

She stared at him wordlessly, well aware that he longed to learn everything there was to know about him; but how could she possibly say so?

Watching her from the depths of an armchair, he queried lazily, 'Are you suggesting we should have a getting-to-know-you session? If so, fire ahead. What would you like to know?'

She hesitated then said, 'Aunt Bea told me that Richard is your only relative...' Too late she saw his jaw tighten and realised that it was an unfortunate beginning.

'That's right. Was it Bea who suggested I expected

to inherit from him, or was that your own brilliant summing-up of the situation?' he demanded with a hint of controlled anger.

'Have you forgotten I've already said I'm sorry for making that particular remark? Or is it that you're an unforgiving type of man?' Looking at him, she really couldn't believe that this was true.

He scowled. 'I'm a man who doesn't forget.'

'You mean you're a man who hangs onto the past—like Brenda.'

'When I get a picture of you in Shaw's arms I see red,' he snarled.

Her eyes filled with pain as she stared at him accusingly. 'You're also a man who likes to hurt.'

'I've been known to hit out at those who hurt others.'

'Very commendable,' she returned, trying to keep the irony from her voice, then wondered what further proof she needed of his continued assumption concerning Garth and herself. 'So, despite your kindness to me, you're also taking great delight in hitting out at me. That's what I call a real contradiction.'

He stared into his glass, his handsome face expressionless as he said, 'We're not making much progress in getting to know each other.'

'Oh, yes, we are. I'm beginning to see you very clearly.' Her voice echoed the sadness filling her thoughts.

'I doubt that you're getting the right impression.' His tone had become clipped, but suddenly it softened as he said, 'Perhaps we could begin again.'

She snatched at the suggestion that might lead to a better relationship. 'Yes, let's do that. Tell me about your childhood.'

'There's little to tell. It was normal until I was fourteen. After that I suddenly grew up.' A shadow of pain crossed his face.

'What happened?' she asked gently, sensing trauma behind his words.

'My parents were killed in a car crash while they

were on holiday. A drunken idiot passed another vehicle and there was a head-on collision with my father's car. After that the rest of my young days were spent at boarding-school, apart from term breaks with Uncle Richard and Aunt Rose, who was alive at that time.'

She tried to edge him away from unhappy memories by saying, 'Tell me about your schooldays before the tragedy. I suppose you were mad on rugby football?'

'Of course. What New Zealand schoolboy isn't? And I was also mad on searching for gold. A schoolfriend named Robert Arrow and I used to haunt the streams and an old mine opening. Brenda often came with us,' he added as an afterthought.

'Your association with Brenda goes back a long way.' Linzi's words came softly as this fact suddenly struck her with force.

'That's right. During those days Dad and Uncle Richard were partners in a land-developing business. Their activities extended over the entire peninsula, although they both lived here at Coromandel.'

Linzi was surprised. 'So you're really a Coromandel man?'

'I suppose you could say so. After leaving school I joined the company with my uncle, but it wasn't long before the job of being an author took over and began to rule my life. That's when I went to live in Auckland,' he said, then fell silent.

She did not disturb his thoughts. Instead her eyes were drawn towards the pale green shirt that did nothing to disguise the contours of his broad shoulders and chest. And from there her gaze slid down to the light fawn trousers that were unable to hide the strength of the long, muscled legs stretching before him. A Coromandel man, she thought again. A man she found to be as fascinating as the district itself with its giant kauri trees, its scarlet pohutukawas and its history of gold.

His voice broke into her thoughts as he went on,

'During my junior years Uncle Richard attended to my parents' estates and to my financial affairs. The money left to me was invested wisely, so I was never in the unhappy state of being a struggling author.'

'You were fortunate to have an uncle like Richard,' she said, recalling the distinguished-looking man who had stood at the altar beside her aunt.

'I'll never forget his kindness to me,' Guy acknowledged, and then, unexpectedly, a flame of anger lit his eyes as he sat upright to snarl at Linzi, 'Believe me, your suspicions *riled* me. The suggestion that I should begrudge Richard his happiness because of what I might miss out on positively got me on the raw. I could have shaken you.'

'I'm—I'm sorry,' she wailed as tears sprang to her eyes. 'How many more times do I have to say it? No doubt this is something else you're unlikely to forget.' The words were flung at him agitatedly as she brushed the moisture away.

'Given time, I might do so,' he gritted.

Honesty compelled her to understand his anger with her, and she turned away dejectedly to stare through the window. The sunset colours had vanished, leaving the sea a mass of dark water and the sky a dull grey. And then another thought struck her. 'I suppose—at school—you were in a dormitory with other boys?'

'Yes. Why do you ask?'

'I was just thinking...' Against the gloom of falling night her imagination saw a row of beds. In one of them a teenage boy lay huddled beneath the blankets, the sheets pressed to his mouth, his thoughts filled with bitterness against the fate that had robbed him of his parents. But—because of other boys in the nearby beds—he did not dare give vent to even a muffled sob. The vision stirred Linzi's emotions to the extent of bringing something that was almost a choking sob into her own throat.

Guy was beside her in a moment, crossing the room to sit on the edge of the settee. 'Hey! What's brought this on? You mustn't cry into your gin. It'll knock the kick out of it.'

'I know I'm being stupid,' she sniffed. 'It was just that I couldn't help thinking of you in that dormitory.'

'Forget it; it's all in the past. I'm a big boy now, in case you haven't noticed.'

'Oh, I've noticed—' She stopped abruptly before she could enlarge upon all that she had noticed about this man who seemed to cause an ache deep inside her.

'Here—take this and have a good blow.' He pressed a clean white handkerchief into her hands. 'And thank you for your sympathy,' he added gruffly. Then as the tears were being mopped he went on, 'Perhaps it was my own trauma of those days that taught me to have a little more sympathy for other people—especially anyone who is obviously unhappy.'

She nodded with understanding. It gave a reason for his kindness towards her, as well as his concern for Brenda. Or was the latter caused by his *love* for Brenda? The thought forced a sigh from her that seemed to come from the depths of her being.

Unexpectedly his hands reached out to grip her shoulders and give her a small shake. 'Snap out of the doldrums.' It was a terse order.

Her face pale, she blinked at the harshness of his tone, then her voice came as a pathetic whisper. 'Somehow I always seem to annoy you. I'm an expert at it.'

'"Annoy"is not the word I'd use,' he returned grimly.

'Perhaps I should've said "frustrate". . .or "madden". It all adds up to one big heap of disapproval,' she quavered.

The grip on her shoulders tightened as he gazed at her wordlessly, his expression enigmatic.

She winced. 'You're hurting me. . .'

'I'm sorry—I didn't mean to.' But instead of releas-ing her his arms enfolded her slim form as he drew her towards him. His hand pressed her head against his shoulder, his fingers moving gently among the auburn waves of her hair.

For several long moments there was a tense silence between them, and although she feared he might become aware of the sledgehammer thumping of her heart she was thankful he'd know nothing of the tingling excitement coursing through her blood. Or would he? Was it possible that he realised just how much the magic of his touch affected her? She closed her eyes before they betrayed these inner secrets.

Slowly, his hand beneath her chin turned her face upwards and towards his own. His head lowered and his sensuous lips claimed her mouth in a kiss that was gently teasing before it became deeper and more possessive.

She felt her stomach muscles tighten as she began to melt into a state of ecstasy, and as the kiss became more passionate it had the effect of lighting a fire somewhere within her body. It was a fire that sent flames of desire shooting through her nerves, making her aware of delicious sensations. Her arms crept about his neck and she clung to him, savouring these precious moments.

But even as she felt the thud of his heart against her own and noticed the quickening of his breath the telephone shrilled through the house. It startled them with a peal that seemed to be louder than usual, almost as though shrieking a warning.

Guy released her abruptly. 'A banshee couldn't do better,' he complained, striding from the room.

His departure left Linzi feeling bereft. A banshee, he'd said. She knew that there were people who believed a banshee to be a female spirit that wailed outside a house to herald a death. Was a woman at the other end of the line? *Brenda?* Was she ringing *again?* If so she'd brought about the sudden death of those precious moments in Guy's arms... And again Linzi was forced to acknowledge to herself that they were precious. And then she found herself consumed with longing to feel his arms about her again.

She could hear his lowered voice in the hall, the deep tones pausing during bouts of listening to the voice coming from the other end. But although she strained her ears she was unable to discern a word being said because most of it sounded like a low, rumbling growl.

Chiding herself, she knew that his conversation was not her business, yet the suspicion that Brenda had rung for the second time that day continued to nag. Therefore she decided to put him to a small test that simmered in her own mind.

If it was somebody other than Brenda, he would return to the settee, but if he was now speaking to Brenda he would not return to continue from where he'd left off. He was not a man who, having just spoken to the woman he loved, would go straight to the arms of another woman. Of this Linzi felt sure.

She waited anxiously, staring at the darkness beyond the window, then gave an involuntary start when he came to the doorway. 'That was Brenda?' Unwillingly the question was dragged from her.

'Yes. She's most unhappy.' There was accusation in the glare he sent across the room.

She felt bewildered, then faltered, 'Why do you look at me like that?'

His mouth gave a slight twist. 'She's unhappy because her husband is like a bear with a sore head. Apparently he's searching for someone he's unable to find. I wonder who that can be?' The final words were snapped curtly.

Linzi forced her shoulders to lift in a small shrug. 'I suppose it's someone he's taken a fancy to,' she returned nervously, her spirits sinking to zero.

'In that case I wonder where she can be?' His words were heavy with sarcasm while he continued to regard her balefully.

She turned away from him, unable to bear the sight of such naked anger. Was this the man who had so recently held her in his arms and kissed her with such passion? It took very little to scratch his veneer, she thought bitterly. A mere phone call from Brenda was sufficient to show that his was only a surface charm.

She felt hurt but resolved that it must not show; therefore she forced a smile as she said lightly, 'It's time we ate. Men are apt to become very cross when they're hungry.'

'At the moment food is not my main concern,' he declared wrathfully. 'Nor is the lack of it making me cross. If you must know the truth I'm feeling really mad with myself.'

'*Yourself?*' His last words amazed her. 'I thought it was only with me. But why also with yourself?'

He began to pace about the room. 'Because I'm allowing this entire issue to affect my work. It interferes with my thoughts.'

She was even more amazed. 'Your *work*? I thought you were boiling over because of Brenda—the one you should've married before she became caught up with Garth Shaw—'

He cut in angrily, 'Heaven give me strength. I'll go and carve the chicken while I'm still sane enough to handle the knife.' He strode from the room.

Linzi flung aside the towel holding the ice-pack to her ankle, then snatched at the crutches lying beside the settee. Moments later she was in the kitchen taking salad foods from the fridge. Little was said during the preparing of the meal, and by the time they sat down she knew that she must make an effort to brush away the dark clouds hovering over their heads.

The long silences were causing her to lose her appetite, although she noticed that Guy did not appear to be suffering from this complaint. Nevertheless he frowned as he ate, and, watching the frown deepen, she decided to try talking in terms of his interests. Casually she queried, 'Have you gathered sufficient photos for your book?'

The question startled him, but at least it dragged his

mind from whatever thoughts had been marring his attractive features. 'Photos? No; I'm afraid the type of photos I want have been difficult to find, while the ones I have found are all so similar that they are not giving me the variety I need to make the book illustrations interesting.' His expression changed to one of doubt as he stared at her. 'Actually, I've been toying with an idea that I now hesitate to put forward.'

'Oh? Why do you hesitate?'

'Because it concerns yourself. You'll probably take great delight in refusing to even think about it,' he stated in a dour tone.

Intrigued, she was unable to prevent a faint smile from touching her lips. 'Refusal is something you're not in the habit of accepting? Is that it?'

'You sound as if you're beginning to know me.'

Her eyes ran over the athletic form now leaning back in the opposite chair. They took in details of the dark hair and brows, then noted the firm line of jaw before coming to rest on the sensuous mouth that had so recently kissed her. The memory of it made her cheeks feel warm, causing her to look away from him as she said, 'I don't presume to know you at all—especially when there are times when you puzzle me. But about this idea you're so sure I'll refuse...why don't you try me and see?'

'OK, I'll lay it on the table. How would you take to the idea of doing sketches to be included in this book? Some could be full-page drawings, while others could occupy space at the ends of chapters. It would be a business commission, of course.'

The suggestion was so unexpected that it made her eyes widen, and for a while she could only stare at him in silence, until at last she said, 'Sketches? What sort of sketches would you need?'

'Anything that applies to the script—such as an old fellow squatting beside a stream while panning for gold, or dirt being washed in a wooden cradle or sluice-box. Nor would sketches of picks, shovels or dirt buckets go amiss. Methods of work were primitive in those days.'

She was still feeling amazed by the request, and after thinking about it for a few minutes she spoke doubtfully. 'I suppose you realise it would lengthen my stay here. I mean. . .it would take longer for you to be rid of me—and isn't that something you desire above all else?' Despite her efforts to keep her voice steady it held a tremor.

His eyes became hooded. 'It might be worth the trauma of having you around. But please understand I wouldn't expect you to begin before you've finished the paintings of the cottage and the old tree out there.'

'And there's another thing. I'd need to read the manuscript,' she warned, recalling his previous aversion to allowing anyone to see his work before it was published.

'Naturally it would be necessary.'

'It would mean that we'd be working in conjunction with each other?' An inner excitement took hold of her as this thought began to register.

'Right. Would that fact worry you too much?'

'No, of course not.' She kept her eyes lowered, fearing they might betray her enthusiasm. *Worry* her? It would send her up into the clouds, and even now the thought of it brought back her appetite sufficiently for her to enjoy her meal. Then, forcing herself to speak casually, she asked, 'When may I see some of the chapters?'

'As soon as you're back on the settee with another ice-pack on your ankle. That's if you're willing to do the job, which is something you've not told me,' he added warily.

'Yes, I'll do it.' She thought for a few moments then sent him a level glance as she said, 'There's just one thing—I shall not take payment for it. Payment will lie in seeing my work published in a book. That wil be reward enough.'

His mouth tightened. 'That might satisfy you, but it

will not satisfy me. I'm not in the habit of accepting charity.'

'I didn't mean it as charity,' she protested with dismay.

'Nor do I intend to be under an obligation to anyone,' he retorted in an unrelenting tone.

She sighed. 'Why must we have so many arguments?'

He drew a hissing breath. 'If you want me to spell it out, it's because there's an underlying rift between us. It's caused by your association with Shaw, which I'm willing to overlook for the moment.'

A gasp of anger escaped her as she blazed, '*You* are willing to overlook—? My oath, that's mighty rich. Let me tell you that the rift between us is caused by *your* persistence in believing Brenda's lies.'

He spoke coldly. 'I've known Brenda for so long that I doubt she'd lie to me. In my own mind I feel she's a truthful person.'

'In your *own mind*...? Huh!' She flung at him furiously. 'Well, it's good to see a man with a mind of his own, *small as it is.*' Then she pulled herself up sharply and muttered an apology. 'I'm sorry, I shouldn't have said that.'

'Apology accepted,' he snapped in a tone that was so chilly it belied the words.

'Thank you, although you could've fooled me,' she returned quietly, while inner distress sent moisture to her eyes, causing her to blink rapidly. Then she went on in a plaintive voice, 'Guy, I don't think this is going to work. I don't think I can do your sketches after all.'

His lips thinned as he frowned at her. 'You're going back on your word *already*?'

She shook her head, searching for a reply. 'It's—it's just that I can't work with such antagonism between us. I think it would be wiser if I did the cottage and the tree as quickly as possible and then returned to Thames.'

His chair scraped the floor as he shoved it back from the table, then he paced about the room before turning to face her. 'Can't we call a truce?' he demanded. 'I'll do my best to keep Shaw's name off the end of my tongue.'

'It's not what you *say*!' she exclaimed bitterly. 'It's what you *think* that frustrates me.'

'You know nothing about frustration,' he rasped. 'Have you ever had to stand by and watch helplessly while someone you're fond of marries a clown?'

It was easy to guess that he was referring to Brenda. 'Then you should've acted while there was still time,' she retorted sharply.

His expression became bleak. 'What can anyone do when a woman declares she loves a man?'

'Nothing, I suppose,' she returned sadly, feeling a depth of sympathy for him. How could Brenda have been so idiotic? How could she have refused this man's love?

Guy spoke imperatively. 'Go into the lounge. I'll bring coffee.' He passed the crutches to her.

'Thank you.' She made her way towards the door but before she reached it he spoke again.

'I'll also bring a couple of chapters for you to read. You can decide whether or not you feel like doing a few sketches to match the script. If you're still adamant about rushing home as soon as possible I'll quite understand.'

She nodded wordlessly.

When she reached the settee she found that the ice-pack was still cold enough to be effective; therefore it was again wrapped to her ankle by the towel. While attending to it she examined the swelling critically, and realised that it was not as bad as it had been; nor was it quite as painful. Thank goodness it was on the mend, she thought with a sigh of relief.

It was enough to make her feel less depressed, and by the time Guy brought the coffee she was sitting comfortably with her leg up and her back resting against the cushions. She was also able to smile cheerfully as he placed the coffee on a small table beside her. 'Thank you,' she murmured gratefully.

'The gloom has lifted?' he queried, regarding her face.

'You could say so. My ankle swelling is going down.'

'Good. Then maybe you'll feel less averse to looking at what I'm doing. I'll fetch the first three chapters.' He left the room, then returned moments later to hand her a sheaf of typed papers.

Linzi took them from him almost reverently. She had never seen the early stages of a book, and now found difficulty in visualising these pages between hard covers. However, she began to read and soon found her interest gripped by the scenes of earlier days.

Guy watched her in silence for several minutes. 'Well?' he demanded at last.

She made no reply. Instead she continued to read, her eyes glued to the page while her mind devoured the thoughts that he had transferred to it.

A smile of satisfaction touched his lips as he left her and went to the kitchen.

Linzi hardly saw him go, and as she turned the pages her mind hovered round suitable sketches. The fluent writing combined descriptions of hardships with patches of humour that made her laugh. It was also sufficiently vivid for her to be able to see the troubles and trials of the earlier miners in their quest for gold. In fact the descriptions were so clear that she knew she had only to make his word pictures visual.

She also knew that it was a task she'd be unable to resist, not only because she was genuinely interested in it but also because it would mean working with Guy. And this, she admitted to herself, was her main reason. Even now his absence from the room made it seem empty.

Watch it, you fool, she warned herself mentally. You have his love for Brenda to contend with. And then she became aware of the jealousy shimmering through her, brought on by the thought of Brenda with her dark hair and flashing dark eyes.

Guy returned as she finished reading the first chapter. He came straight to the point with an uncompromising demand that seemed to fit his dominating character. 'Well, what is your decision? Is it to be the sketches, or home to Thames without sparing the horses?'

'I—I think I'll enjoy doing the sketches.' Better not sound too eager, she decided.

'You will? That's a promise?' He eyed her keenly, as though searching for doubts.

She nodded. 'Yes, but I must finish the two paintings first.' Any other paintings for the exhibition she had in mind would have to wait, she decided.

Guy took the remaining pages from her. 'There'll be plenty of time to read these later,' he said. 'Just now I need to show my gratitude for your decision to stay and do the job.'

He sat on the edge of the settee and took her in his arms again. His lips found hers, and it was almost as though there had been no interruption to the last time he'd kissed her. . .no phone call with Brenda at the other end.

As the kiss deepened she made no effort to remain calm by reminding herself that this embrace was due to nothing more than gratitude. He'd said so, hadn't he? But despite the warning she issued to herself her heart thumped and her breath quickened as a wild exhilaration sent curious twinges into her abdomen. Nor did her arms listen to her brain. Of their own volition they crept about his neck, her fingers fondling the dark hair at the back of his head. And as she felt her breasts pressed against the hardness of his chest she knew that her nipples had become taut.

It seemed as though Guy also knew that her nipples had turned into miniature rosebuds, and as though answering a call his hand moved to slip beneath the neckline of her dress. It cupped the fullness of her soft breast, the gentle stroking of his thumb causing uncontrolled whimpers of pleasure to escape her.

She clung to him as his lips left her mouth to trace a line of small kisses from her brow and closed lids down to her cheeks and throat, where they found a vulnerable pulse. But even as unfamiliar sensations made her tremble with desire she was assailed by the memory of that word 'gratitude'. It stabbed at her mind, changing her murmurs of delight into sudden protests as she gripped his wrist in an effort to remove his hand from her breast. 'Please. . .please stop,' she gasped. 'This is getting out of hand.'

He complied reluctantly, having planted a final kiss on her throat. 'You're right,' he admitted huskily, taking in every detail of her flushed face. 'You can thank your ankle that it hasn't gone further. Lovemaking must not be restricted by twinges of pain.'

The rosiness of her face deepened. 'Aren't you taking a lot for granted?' she demanded tremulously.

'I don't think so. Your response told me. . .a little. But have no fear; in future I'll keep myself strictly under control.'

She stared at him wordlessly, the colour draining from her face as she realised exactly how much he would have been able to read into her response. It would have told him that she'd revelled in being in his arms. . .and that she had longed for more than mere kisses. It would have betrayed that she was ready and willing to give herself to him there and then, on the settee or on the floor. If it hadn't been for that word 'gratitude' *it might have happened.*

Watching the expression on her face, he said, 'You're taking this far too seriously. Why don't you just forget it? It won't happen again.'

She continued to stare at him in silence, a sudden chill sweeping through her body until it settled somewhere within the region of her heart. Did those words mean that he was rejecting her? Then pride asserted itself as she said in a flat tone, 'You bet it won't happen again. Now perhaps you'll allow me to finish reading those pages.'

'Sure. Go ahead.' He stood up abruptly and left the room.

She lifted the pages from where they had been placed on the small table beside the settee, but although she stared at them the words failed to register. Twice her eyes returned to the top of the page, but at last, feeling thoroughly despondent, she laid her papers in her lap then closed her eyes, leaning her head against a cushion on the arm of the settee. After that the tears gathered, and as they trickled down her cheeks they did much to wash away her tension, thus enabling her to pull her emotions into some sort of order.

She was being a fool, she chided herself mentally. As Guy had said, she was taking this far too seriously. She'd be much wiser to forget it—*if she could*— because, obviously, *he* intended to do exactly that.

And proof of that seemed to live in the fact that he spent the rest of the evening at his word processor.

Later, while lying in bed, she made a firm resolution. She would not allow this man to get under her skin, much less into her system. In future she would look upon him as a casual acquaintance, and when this period at Kauri Cottage was over they would both follow their separate paths. She would go her way and he would go his. And that would be that.

CHAPTER SIX

LINZI's resolve was still strong when she woke next morning, and added to it was the knowledge that the sooner she completed the tasks before her, the sooner she would be able to leave Guy Nelson to his desired solitude and his thoughts of Brenda.

Fortunately there was a further improvement in her ankle, although when she tested it on the floor she realised that the time had not yet come to discard the crutches. She dressed in a pair of navy and white shorts with a matching blouse, and when she went to the kitchen she discovered that Guy was already at work in the dining room.

Dishes on the bench indicated that he'd had breakfast at an earlier hour, and she wondered if he wished to avoid her. She stared at his empty chair and was overcome by a feeling of loneliness that was so intense that she was forced to remind herself that this was not the way to get him out of her mind.

And then she came to a decision. This morning she would not work out of doors. Instead she would set up her easel in the third bedroom and work on the area of sky and sea that would form the background for the pohutukawa tree. By doing so she would escape the need to seek Guy's assistance in carrying her equipment outside. If he wished to avoid her, so be it. She would also avoid him.

Dejectedly, she forced herself to eat a breakfast of tea, toast and marmalade—only because she knew that it was wise to do so. Then, after clearing the table and bench, she went to the bedroom studio where she put on a grey smock that was well daubed with oil paint.

As usual the excitement of beginning on a new canvas began to take hold, and her spirits lifted as she

95

squeezed small amounts of cobalt-blue, cerulean, yellow ochre, light red and white onto her clean palette. Her palette knife was then used to mix the desired hues for sky and clouds, and after that the time passed quickly until suddenly Guy's voice made her jump.

He sounded cross, and she turned to see him scowling at her from the doorway, his scanty attire against the heat of the day making her catch her breath. Almost mesmerised, she could only stare in silence at the broad chest with its mat of crisp dark hairs which were revealed by a white shirt that lay open to the waist, and at his long, muscular legs, bare below the grey shorts.

'Why didn't you ask me to carry your paint-box and easel outside for you?' he demanded tersely.

She glanced out of the window where the waving branches of trees gave her an answer. 'It was too windy,' she informed him calmly. 'I dislike sudden gusts blowing a canvas covered with wet paint against my face.'

'I see.' The reply appeared to placate him. 'I thought you were still boiled up because of that kiss.'

'Oh, no... As you suggested, I've forgotten about it,' she lied, turning away from him and continuing to work on the canvas.

'Perhaps it's just as well.' He watched her soften the edges of the clouds then added, 'I'm about to make coffee. I'll bring you a mug.'

She sent him a radiant smile. 'Thank you. To be honest, I'm ready for it.' Then she returned to the clouds.

If she had been even more honest she would have admitted to feeling relieved that their relationship was sliding back onto an even keel, and suddenly it seemed as though last night's incident with its moments of passion had never happened. As he had said, she was taking the affair far too seriously, and when he returned with the coffee she was able to match his own casual attitude while sipping gratefully.

Yet despite her outer nonchalance she was painfully conscious of his presence, and although he did not touch her he stood close enough for her to be aware of the tangy fragrance of his aftershave. And even that was enough to make the feeling of tenseness come surging back. However, he did not remain in the room for long, and although she regretted seeing him leave she told herself that it was a relief...which was another lie.

However, he had been gone for only a few moments before he returned to the door, his expression quizzical as he said, 'High tide will be at noon. I thought we could go for a swim. I presume you've brought a swimsuit with you?'

'I never come here without one—although at the moment it would be difficult for me to get to the water,' she added ruefully.

He grinned then drawled smoothly, 'I dare say we can overcome that small problem, so long as you'll risk allowing me to help you into the surf.' His tone was so full of mockery that there was even a laugh attached to it.

'Yes, of course,' she mumbled, feeling unable to meet his eyes.

'It'll mean using your crutches as far as the stony area, and then I'll carry you down to the water.' The hazel eyes were full of mischief as they glinted at her.

She nodded, unable to speak because the memory of his mocking laugh continued to niggle at her. In a subtle way it told her that he *knew* she was affected by him...and that she'd *adore* being swept up into his arms and carried down to the surf.

He went on, 'We'll enjoy a dip before lunch. We'll go down at midday and eat at one o'clock.' The words came with the emphasis of one who had made up his mind, then he left the room.

Shall we indeed, Mr Nelson? she thought furiously while gripping the long, slim paintbrush until it almost snapped. We'll see about *that*. He had not bothered to ask if the time would be suitable for her, she noticed with growing irritation. He had simply stated what they would do and had expected her to fall in with his plans.

And then the thought of being carried down to the water made concentration difficult, despite the fact that she assured herself it was no big deal. Yet it *was* a big deal because it was almost as if he'd told her he could pick her up or put her down whenever it pleased him to do so. It seemed to suggest that he looked upon her as a lump of soft clay, ready and willing to be moulded against him whenever he desired. It also implied that without him she couldn't go far. At least, not at the moment.

'He's wrong,' she mumbled at the clouds on the canvas. 'I'll get there under my own steam, even if I have to crawl. And as for waiting until midday...no sir—I'll go at eleven-thirty.' After that she kept an eye on the time.

At eleven-fifteen a glance into the passage showed the dining-room door to be firmly closed. Staring at it bleakly, she read the message which seemed to tell her to keep out. 'OK, Mr Nelson, I'll do just that,' she muttered, making silent progress towards her bedroom.

It took only a few minutes to remove the ankle bandage and to climb into her purple bikini, which was the least revealing one she had been able to buy. Even so the fitted top betrayed the soft fullness of her rounded breasts, while the high-cut briefs made her legs look long. Lastly she slipped her arms into a white towelling wrap and tied the belt about her waist.

Opening the bedroom door a fraction, she peered out to make sure that the dining-room door was still closed; then, making as little sound as possible, she left the cottage by the front entrance.

Progress along the drive and across the road was easy, but difficulties arose when she reached the hazardous area of beach gravel and stones. The latter rolled beneath the pressure of her crutches, causing them to slip and throw her off balance. However, she pressed on with dogged determination, telling herself that it would be easier when she reached the sand.

But that was not the case because the sand was dry and soft, and, instead of sliding, her crutches now sank in deeply and failed to support her weight. She fell to her knees and, frustrated, took off the towelling wrap, laid her cruches on top of it, then crawled the rest of the way.

Soon she was floating on her back in water that sparkled as it soothed her nerves and even removed the ache from her ankle. But as it lapped against her shoulders she knew that something was missing. It was human presence. She was alone. And then she recalled her father saying that nothing was any good unless it was shared. And, even if she had asserted herself where Guy was concerned, she knew she'd been stupid to come without him, because this lonely swim was giving her no joy at all.

A short time later he arrived with a face like thunder. And then his voice hit her ears. 'If you had no desire to swim with me, why couldn't you have said so?' he roared above the sound of the waves breaking on the beach.

'It wasn't that,' she said, becoming vitally aware of the latent power in his tanned, muscular body.

'Then what was it?' he demanded, arriving at her side.

'You wouldn't understand.' She turned away from him and began to swim seawards.

He followed her, taking only a few strokes to reach her, and then his hand on her shoulder turned her to face him. 'You didn't want to be carried. . .was that it? You wouldn't accept my help.'

'It was the taunting way in which you offered,' she flung at him, then wondered why the sight of this man continued to make her pulses race.

'OK, so you don't want my help. Message received and understood,' he rasped. Then, as he watched her turn and begin to swim further out, he shouted furiously, 'Don't go out too far. I've no intention of dragging you back from the middle of the Hauraki Gulf...'

His words came faintly, and although they registered they merely kindled a flame of defence in Linzi. She was a good swimmer, but had no intention of going out too far, so how dared he assume she would act so stupidly? Stretching herself, she began to swim with strong, steady strokes.

Moments later he was beside her, his fingers gripping her arm with the force of iron clamps. His expression irate, he shouted, 'Didn't you hear what I said? Suppose you get cramp while out here alone, or meet something with jaws and a triangular fin poking out of the water? There now—*take a look*.'

She turned to stare in the direction he pointed and was in time to see a dark, curved shape rise and then disappear. A shriek of horror escaped her as she set off for the shore, her arms and legs working frantically as she swam with all the speed she could muster. Vaguely, she was aware of the ache in her ankle, but it was ignored, and at last she lay panting at the water's edge while wavelets washed over her.

When Guy came to lie beside her she stared at him with eyes that were still filled with panic. 'Was that really a shark?' she quavered.

He grinned at her, his teeth flashing whitely in his tanned face. 'No. That was a porpoise. They're friendly fellows.'

Her terror evaporated as she sat up and glared at him. 'But you made me believe it was a *shark*. You came up with all that talk about jaws and—and fins.'

He lay on his side, his eyes wandering slowly from her cleavage to her slim waist. 'It *could* have been a mako shark or a hammerhead. There are at least a dozen species of shark basking round our shores.'

Her eyes blazed with anger as she ranted accusingly, 'You *knew* it was only a porpoise, yet you *deliberately* frightened the living daylights out of me.'

He nodded, then admitted without the slightest sign of remorse, 'Yes. I had to scare the hell out of you. It was the easiest and quickest way of getting you back to safer waters without a lot of argument. It was just luck that the porpoise happened to be there at the right moment, although they're often in this bay.'

'They are? How do you know that, Mr Know-all?'

'You're forgetting I grew up round these parts. Didn't I tell you I'm a Coromandel man?'

'Yes, you did—but I'm still unable to see that such extreme measures were necessary,' she complained, allowing her eyes to roam over the glistening wetness of the almost naked body lying beside her among the gently breaking ripples. He's magnificent, she thought, and every inch a man, wherever he's come from. And, dragging her eyes away from the broad chest, she also knew that he was a man she would never forget.

His voice came drily. 'Extreme measures are usually necessary when one comes up against stubborn female perversity.'

'Are you suggesting I'm pigheaded?' she demanded sharply.

'That's your word, not mine. However, if the glove fits you'd be wise to slap yourself with it.' The words were uttered with a smile that did not really reach his eyes.

She felt stung. 'You sound as if you think I'm a thoroughly ungrateful person.'

'Well, aren't you?'

She thought of the crutches he'd acquired for her. 'Of course not. I appreciate the help you've given me, and I'm sorry for the interruption it has caused to your work.'

His hazel eyes gleamed with a challenge. 'Then prove it. Kiss me on the cheek and say, Thank you, Guy.'

She was startled by the request, but she knew it would be ungracious to refuse. Nor did she have any wish to do so, and after a rapid glance had assured her of the emptiness of the beach and of the distance of the nearest houses she leaned forward to brush her lips across his cheek.

But they never got that far because his arms shot out and dragged her against the length of his body. The feel of his bare skin against her own threw her senses into orbit, and as his mouth fastened upon hers her arms clung to him of their own volition.

As the kiss deepened she knew that his heart pounded in unison with her own. She felt his breath become ragged, and as his hands slid down her body to hold her even closer she dissolved into something as pliable as soft butter. It was impossible to mistake the extent of his longing to make love. It reached the depths of her soul by sending tremors of delicious sensations pulsating through her entire being, causing her to arch against him without realising that she was doing so.

But suddenly it ended as he tore his mouth from hers and muttered a ferocious, 'Damn—that wasn't meant to happen.' His hands left her body to pull her arms from about his neck with a decisive movement, then he leapt to his feet and raced into the surf.

The action stunned her, and for several long moments she lay shivering with an icy chill that the sun was unable to remove. It was the second time he had rejected her, and the knowledge wrapped her in a cloak of humiliation.

'OK, Mr Nelson, *see if I care*,' she shouted at the man diving through the roll of a breaking wave, feeling confident that he was unable to hear her. 'Believe me, it won't happen again,' she added, glaring in his direction. But one thing was definite—she had to get away from this place, although first the two paintings had to be finished as well as the promised sketches. So why was she wasting time lying about on this beach? she asked herself angrily.

She rolled over and crawled to where she'd left her crutches, then shrugged herself into the towelling wrap. She guessed that Guy watched her progress towards the stony area, and she could almost imagine the grin of amusement on his face.

However, she did not look back, and nor did he come to help her. Had he done so, would she have refused his assistance? It was a question she was unable to answer even to herself because pride was fighting with the longing to be lifted up into his arms. And the more she thought about the matter, the more confused she became.

Yet, strangely, by the time she had made her laborious way home the anger she was struggling to hold against Guy had vanished. And the fact that she was feeling hungry after the swim made her realise that he would be ravenous.

A quick shower washed the sand and salt from her skin, and as the waves of her auburn hair dried they fluffed about her head like a shining bronze halo which caught lights from the yellow shorts and blouse she put on.

In the kitchen she went to the freezer where she searched for the savoury quiche that Aunt Bea always kept ready for unexpected lunch guests. It consisted of sweetcorn, bacon, grated cheese and red peppers, and as she placed it in the oven Linzi hoped that Guy would enjoy it. And then she stood still, wondering at herself. Why was she so anxious to have a meal ready for when he returned from his swim? Why was she so concerned about whether or not he'd enjoy it? Was she in love with him? No. . .definitely not. She shied away from the thought.

Yet there had to be a reason for the effect he had upon her. No other man had called to her with such crystal clarity; no other man had made her flesh tingle with a single touch. Nor had any other man made her ready to lie in his arms and give more than mere kisses. This last thought caused her to draw a sharp breath as she admitted the truth to herself. Yes. . *she loved him.*

The knowledge left her feeling shaken, and it also sent her to the front veranda to see if he appeared to be coming home. But there was no sign of him, and although she fetched her aunt's binoculars to scan the beach and sea he was not to be seen. This is ridiculous; he must be out there *somewhere*, she thought, becoming conscious of a fear that intensified with every passing moment.

Despite his warning to her, had he himself swum out too far and then suffered from cramp? Had the porpoise turned out to be a shark after all? The thought filled her with horror, causing her hands to shake as they held the binoculars. Her vision became blurred as tears filled her eyes, rolling down her cheeks while she wondered what she should do.

Should she call the police, who would no doubt take ages to reach here? How long has he been missing? they'd ask. Only since about one o'clock, she'd have to admit. They'd look at her and laugh, but she would have done her best. More tears blinded her as she went to the phone, and she had almost reached it when she heard the back door open and close.

She fled into her bedroom and shut the door, then listened as Guy went to the bathroom and turned on the shower. Feeling almost sick with relief, she pulled herself together, then dabbed at her eyes and blew her nose before attending to the damage with make-up. 'You *stupid* fool,' she hissed at herself in the mirror.

A short time later the quiche had heated sufficiently to eat, and as Linzi served it with a hastily prepared salad she said casually, 'You were out there a long time. I was beginning to wonder if you were examining the sandy bottom.'

'On the contrary, I came out soon after watching you struggle home. Refusing my help must have given you much satisfaction.' His tone was sardonic.

She looked at him reproachfully. So he *had* observed her difficult progress across the stony areas. But she merely asked, 'Where have you been all this time?'

'Sunbathing in a sheltered spot at the back of the house. And incidentally, your place at the manuka bushes is also sheltered, so if you wish to continue with the cottage painting I'll see you settled there.' His voice became noticeably harder. 'Whether you like it or not, I shall carry your things there. Is that understood, or do you still intend to make a fuss about accepting my assistance?'

She stared at her plate while speaking humbly. 'Thank you, Guy. I'll be thankful for your help.'

'Good. Common sense at last.' He continued to regard her with eyes that were penetrating. 'Now perhaps you'll tell me why you've been weeping.'

She raked about in her mind for a reply, but was unable to come up with anything more suitable than, 'Can't a girl shed a few tears without having to explain them?'

'I suppose it's permissible...although you're no longer a girl. You're every inch a woman, and a most attractive one, I might add.'

'Thank you,' she said in a small voice, glowing inwardly.

The hazel eyes continued to hold questions as he probed with persistence, 'Did I embarrass you down on the beach? Did you fear I intended to force you to make love there and then?'

She felt her cheeks become hot as they turned a deep red. 'No, of course not—'

'Not that there would've been much forcing,' he went on relentlessly. 'I know you wanted me every bit as much as I wanted you. Perhaps you've been weeping because it didn't happen.'

She turned away, unable to meet his eyes as she pleaded, 'Please stop talking like this. It's not something I wish to discuss.'

'OK, but I'll say just one thing more. When we make love it won't be down on the beach within sight of hillside houses, however distant they happen to be.'

More colour flooded into her face as a gasp escaped her. 'When we— My oath, you've got a nerve. What gives you the temerity to even imagine I'd allow you to satisfy your male needs with my body?'

'Don't make any error—it'll happen,' he responded quietly.

'That's what *you* think,' she snapped furiously, realising that there was no love for herself involved here. It was merely a case of a man hoping to make love with a woman he happened to find attractive. And, conscious as she was of her own feelings towards him, the knowledge was like a knife wound. But, after all, what else could she expect? Here was a man with a deeply rooted conviction that she had had an affair with Garth Shaw; therefore he had little or no respect for her, much less any real love. But that wouldn't stop him from *using* her, she reasoned.

Fighting against more tears, she left the table and went to the third bedroom, where she prepared to take the cottage painting out of doors. However, she had scarcely folded her easel and closed her paint-box before Guy was beside her, gathering the things she needed. She then followed meekly while he strode ahead towards the shelter of the brush-like branches of the manuka bushes.

Little was said apart from her few mumbled words of thanks, and as she watched him stride away she wondered what had made her imagine that she loved this man. Yet she knew that she did. She sighed and began mixing a colour for the shadowed areas of the cottage.

An hour later she was working steadily when she realised that the wind had dropped and that ominous dark clouds had gathered in the western sky. They heralded rain, which would prevent her from working outside, and she knew that while the sun still gave the contrasts of lights and shadows a photo of the subject must be taken.

But the Polaroid camera which took instant prints had been left indoors, and she had no option but to fetch it before the clouds gathered overhead. Impatient with herself for having forgotten to bring it outside, she reached for her crutches and made her way back to the cottage.

As she entered the back door she heard Guy's voice. He was on the phone, his words reaching Linzi as she paused in the kitchen.

'My dear girl, I find that very hard to believe,' he said, then replaced the receiver as Linzi stepped into the passageway.

She noticed a strained expression cross his face, but it was so fleeting that she wondered if she had imagined it; therefore she forced herself to smile as she said, 'Your dear girl. . . It must be Brenda again.'

A steely glint crept into his eyes, but he ignored her comment and rasped, 'You forgot something?'

She was startled by his tone but replied in a calm voice, 'Yes, my Polaroid camera. I use it to snap interesting subjects I'm unable to sketch just at that moment, and it also gives me a record for the sake of accuracy. It's wonderful the way it prints the picture only moments after it has been taken.' She went on to explain why she thought she should photograph the cottage, and as she spoke she became consumed by curiosity. What was he finding so hard to believe? Did it concern herself?

In an effort to find out she said unguardedly, 'Poor Brenda. . . Why does she persist in phoning you? Is it for your sympathy, or just to hear your voice? She must be a very unhappy person. . .' Her voice trailed away as the anger on his face caused her to fall silent.

'Yes, I'm afraid so.' Then he stepped closer to stare down into her face with a long, hard look that held accusation. 'Do you normally listen in on the conversations of other people?' he demanded in a voice like granite. 'How long were you standing in the kitchen eavesdropping?'

She was taken aback by his obvious contempt. Her chin rose and her face became flushed as she glared at him. 'How dare you suggest I would do so?' she retaliated. 'I have only just come in.'

'Yet you appear to have heard what I said.'

'I heard only the last of what you said to your—your *married* girlfriend.' The words were spat at him as jealousy seized her.

His jaw tightened as he snarled, 'What are you hinting at?'

Her eyes flashed with blue-green sparks. 'It's exactly the same hint that you persist in throwing at me.'

'You're forgetting that I don't need to hint,' he gritted. 'I have the evidence of seeing you in Shaw's arms, whereas you have nothing to go on as far as Brenda and I are concerned.'

Linzi gave a derisive laugh. 'Nothing? Huh! Then why does she continue to phone you?'

He frowned thoughtfully. 'I really don't know... unless, as an old friend, she feels I'm someone in whom she can confide.'

Linzi gave a scornful laugh. 'Don't you mean you have an understanding ear into which she can pour vitriol?'

His eyes narrowed as he accused softly, 'I believe you heard more than you care to admit.'

She shook her head. 'No, but it's easy to guess that I featured in that conversation. Tell me, what was it you found so hard to believe?' The question was accompanied by a smile which, Linzi hoped, might ease the tension between them.

But Guy did not give her an answer. He left her abruptly and went into the dining room, shutting the door behind him with more force than was necessary.

It had almost been slammed in her face, she thought miserably. It was almost as though he'd told her to mind her own damned business—and that, she supposed, was what she should be doing. Yet her curiosity continued to nag at her, especially when she recalled the peculiar look that had flashed into Guy's eyes as she had entered the passage.

At the time she had thought little of it, but now it seemed to confirm that she *had* featured in the phone conversation, although that was mere conjecture, she argued with herself. She had no proof, nor had Guy admitted it to be a fact. And then the thought of the gathering clouds sent her hastening to find her camera before the sun disappeared and took away the all-important shadows that gave form to an otherwise flat scene.

Several minutes later, with the camera slung over her shoulder, she was heading back towards her easel when she was struck by the uncanny feeling of being watched. She stopped abruptly, and, swinging round to stare at the cottage, she was in time to see a movement at the dining-room window.

It told her that Guy had stood watching her progress, and the knowledge drove home the fact that once again she was taking his mind from his work—so it was little wonder that he was continually cross with her. But she wasn't the only one, she argued silently. Brenda, with her persistent phone calls, was doing her share of disturbing his concentration.

Back at her easel the photo was taken, and when the print slid out of the front of the camera she breathed a sigh of gratitude for modern technology. But when she settled down to continue with her painting she found her own concentration completely shattered by visions of those erotic moments on the beach. In some intangible way his charisma reached out to engulf her, causing a wave of longing for those delicious moments to be repeated.

Again she felt the strength of his arms as he'd clasped her against his lean and powerful body, which had been almost naked except for his brief swimming trunks. And then the memory of his manhood pressing against her bikini-clad form set her on fire. Her hand holding the paintbrush trembled to such an extent that she was unable to control her brush strokes, and she had no option but to cease her efforts while trying to regain her composure.

Her memory leapt to his words in the kitchen. 'When we make love it won't be down on the beach within sight of hillside houses, however distant. . .' he'd said. Did that mean he intended to come to her bed? she wondered with sudden fear for her ability to resist him. If only there were a key to the door she'd feel less danger from the intensity of her own longing.

Eventually the importance of capturing the shadows of the cottage forced her mind to become more controlled, and she was attending to their depths when the first drops of rain splashed on the canvas. She looked up at the dark clouds overhead and, realising that there was more rain to come, closed her box, folded her easel and prepared to take her things indoors.

She knew she should call for Guy's help, but a streak of stubborn independence prevented her from doing so. She would move her things inside alone, even if it meant carrying them one by one and making several trips through the rain.

She was struggling to manipulate the painting and her crutches at the same time when Guy came striding from the cottage.

'I saw the spits of rain on the window,' he said, taking the folded easel from her and tucking it under his arm. Then, grasping the handle of her paint-box, he demanded, 'Am I right in assuming you had no intention of asking for my help?'

'I didn't wish to disturb you,' she mumbled, feeling thankful that he had arrived. 'You've had so much disturbance from me. . .as well as from other people.' The last words just slipped out.

'Other people? I'm unaware there's anyone else around.'

'They haven't had to be present to be on your mind,' she pointed out bleakly as they went towards the cottage.

'Ah, I presume you're referring to Brenda. Then

hear this: if Brenda wishes to pour her troubles into the ear of an old friend, surely the least I can do is listen and offer comfort? Or is that too much for you to understand?' he rasped impatiently.

'Of course not. If Brenda is unhappy I feel sorry for her, so please don't think I'm unsympathetic towards her situation of being married to Garth.'

'Do you mean those words? You really are sorry for her?' He looked at her eagerly, as though hoping she felt genuine sympathy for the woman who had been his friend for so long.

She looked at him earnestly. 'Believe me, I'd feel sorry for *anyone* who was married to Garth Shaw, even if that person had humiliated and told lies about me. I can even forgive her.'

'I'm glad about that,' he said softly, his eyes kindling as he looked at her. 'I'd like you to be more friendly with Brenda.'

His words caused her to laugh. 'You've got to be joking.'

He remained serious. 'Why should I joke? Why shouldn't I mean what I say?'

Her amusement turned to incredulity. 'I can hardly believe I'm hearing this. Nor can I understand why the relationship between Brenda and myself should matter to you.'

'It's simply that I like my friends to be amicable towards each other. It's always so much easier when we meet, especially at social gatherings. Surely that makes sense to you?' he queried with one dark brow raised.

'I suppose it does. . .except that you and I will be unlikely to meet, especially as you live in Auckland,' Linzi reminded him.

He hesitated then admitted, 'To be honest, I've been considering moving to Thames.'

'I see.' Linzi sent him a level glance. 'To be nearer to Brenda, I presume?'

'Wrong. To be nearer to my uncle. In future I mean

to keep in closer touch with him. I'm very fond of him, and now that I'm established it's not imperative for me to live in Auckland, or to be close to my publisher.' Guy paused, then sent her a direct stare as he said, 'I shall also keep in contact with you.'

Her heart leapt at the words. 'I—I thought you'd be glad to see the back of me.'

His eyes remained hooded as he said, 'You're forgetting about the sketches in the book. You'll need to give your approval to the proofs.'

'Oh, I hadn't thought of that. It's so new to me.'

'When the book is published I dare say we'll have a launch party in Thames. I wouldn't like to see it ruined through a showing of feline claws.' His voice held a warning.

'Then you'd be wise to send the message in the right direction,' Linzi retorted sharply, resenting his suggestion that she would be the cause of any trouble that could arise.

Nothing further was said until they reached the cottage, and by that time the spits of rain had developed into a light shower. They entered the bedroom-cum-studio in a slightly damp state, and as Linzi watched Guy erect the easel she attempted to change the subject that had previously occupied their minds.

'I used my camera just in time,' she said, handing him the print of the cottage which showed details of highlights and strong shadows.

He examined it critically, then commented, 'It's an excellent photo. Your camera appears to be one of the more expensive Polaroids.'

'Yes. It was a gift.' She smiled happily, recalling the day it had been given to her.

He watched her with narrowed eyes, his jaw tightening as he queried, 'A gift from a person I happen to know?'

She caught his meaning. 'It was not from the person your mind is so quick to suspect,' she returned coldly.

'Who says I suspect anyone?' he hedged.

'I do. Suspicion is sticking out of your ears. You're more than ready to believe that Garth has been showering me with gifts.' She opened the case to show him a small card stuck inside the lid.

His face cleared as he read it aloud. '"Happy birthday, darling. Love from Mum and Dad."'

Linzi spoke briskly. 'Now then, we'd better change from these damp clothes, otherwise we'll be in bed with colds.'

Guy grinned. 'Dare I hope that you mean *together*?'

CHAPTER SEVEN

GUY's last words echoed in Linzi's mind as she went to her bedroom. They were words that held a depth of meaning for her—but for *him* they appeared to hold little more than amusement.

Perhaps it was the word 'together' that had had such impact, she decided. Her parents were very much a 'together' couple whose love for each other was obvious, and the knowledge that she would never attain that state of union with Guy made her feel sad.

A sigh escaped her as she changed back into the navy and white shorts and blouse she'd worn that morning, and when she went back to the third bedroom she saw that the dining-room door had been firmly closed. OK, Guy, message received, she thought, realising he wished for no further disturbance. After all, he'd come here for solitude and silence in which to work, and he'd had exactly that until it had been shattered by her own arrival.

She worked solidly until it was time to prepare the evening meal, but even then she saw him only briefly because as soon as he had finished eating he disappeared once more into the dining room. And again the door was closed.

She walked past it to the front veranda where she stood staring at the heavy clouds and falling rain, which did nothing to lift her feeling of gloom. Restlessly, she wondered how to fill in the dreary evening, knowing that at heart she was longing for Guy's company.

But that was something denied her; therefore should she return to the third bedroom and give the cottage its final brush strokes? No. She needed a rest from it, and in any case it was wiser to complete it in the daylight. She also knew that TV in the lounge was out of the question because the distracting sound would float through the wall to the dining room.

There was only one thing to do, she decided at last. She would go to bed and read. And, making her way to the bookshelf in her aunt's bedroom, she decided to choose a romance. If she couldn't find romance in her own life, she might find it in the pages of a book, she thought sadly, preparing to get between the sheets.

Two hours later she was still sitting up with pillows at her back. The story had held her engrossed from the first page, clearing away her own mental frustrations while presenting the problems of other people. Strangely, the sound of rain on the roof was now comforting rather than depressing. And then came the added sound of an unexpected knock on the door. . .

Startled, she called, 'Come in.' Then as Guy put his head round the door she said thoughtlessly, 'Oh, it's you. . .'

He grinned, then said facetiously, 'Who were you expecting—the milkman?'

Thank heavens he hadn't said Garth Shaw, she thought with a sense of relief, then explained, 'I'm afraid I was lost in my book.'

He said, 'Would you like a mug of chocolate? I reached the stage of needing something, and when I saw the light under your door I guessed you were reading.' The door was then pushed further open and he came in with a small tray on which were two steaming mugs.

Linzi looked at him gratefully. 'Thank you, I'd love it.'

Suddenly conscious of her revealing nightdress, she sat up while pulling the bedclothes beneath her chin. Had his previous anger towards her vanished? she wondered with a slight quickening of breath. If so, she also felt grateful for that particular mercy.

Or had he something further in mind? Was that hot chocolate just a preliminary gesture of friendship that would open the door to the lovemaking that he had declared would occur? Had that time come now? Staring into the mug, she made an effort to control the fluttering of her nerves.

Guy sat on the side of the bed. He appeared to be in a thoughtful mood, and if he noticed that holding the mug had caused the blankets to slip sufficiently to reveal Linzi's bare shoulders he gave no sign of it. Nor did he even glance at her as he said, 'I've been thinking about your camera.'

The words came as an anticlimax. 'My—my *camera*?' she echoed, having felt sure that he'd had something very different in mind.

'I thought we might use it tomorrow.'

'You mean out in the rain? It seems to be set in.' She looked at him incredulously, then sent a glance at the water trickling down the darkened window.

He gave a snort of impatience. 'No, *not* out in the rain. Thank you for considering me to be a nutcase. I mean we could take photos in a small museum where there is memorabilia of the gold-mining days. It would make your task of doing the sketches for my book so much easier, if you get my meaning.'

'And so much quicker,' she said. 'It would hasten my departure. Oh, yes. . . I get your meaning.'

'That's not what I had in mind,' he growled.

She smiled, then uttered a small, shaky laugh. 'You're sure about that?'

'How can you doubt it?'

'Very easily, mainly because you're continually so cross with me. Every time Brenda phones you our—our association deteriorates a little further.' She paused as a thought struck her, then asked casually, 'Incidentally, does she know I'm here—alone in the cottage with you?'

'Of course not,' he snapped.

'Why haven't you told her? Why haven't you declared you'll thrash me within an inch of my life unless I promise to stop chasing her husband?' The thought of herself pursuing Garth Shaw struck her as being so humorous that she began to shake with laughter.

But Guy did not find it amusing. Scowling, he spoke from between tight lips. 'I'm glad you think it's funny. Personally, I don't. *Personally*, I find the entire situation to be a pain in the neck. I came to this cottage to work in peace and without the hassles of interruption. But what else do I find?'

She felt contrite, knowing that she herself had contributed to part of that interference to his work, and her voice was sincere with apology as she said, 'I'm sorry about my ankle causing me to become a pest. . . and I do appreciate the help you've given in carrying things for me. . .but your *real* trouble has been mental anxiety caused by Brenda.'

He frowned. 'That's a load of rubbish.'

She shook her head. 'No, it's not rubbish. Brenda has a plan. She's using me as a scapegoat in her efforts to get closer to you, but you are too blind to see it.'

'You've got to be joking,' he snorted angrily.

'Indeed I am not, otherwise why would she keep phoning *you*? Why not cry on her *parents'* shoulders?' And, having voiced the words, Linzi became convinced that they were a fact; therefore she went on, 'If you're still in love with her you have only to open your arms. She'll fly into them like a bird returning to its nest.'

'Leaving you and Shaw free to get together?' he snarled. 'Are you sure this isn't *wishful thinking* on your part?' He placed his empty mug on the small bedside table with a slight bang, then ran long fingers through his dark hair in an impatient gesture. It was almost as though the thought angered him more than he cared to admit.

'Wishful thinking. . .' Linzi scoffed scornfully, her eyes blazing with sudden anger. 'You must be out of your mind.' Glaring at him she realised the futility of trying to convince him of the true situation between herself and Garth Shaw. Then a deep sigh escaped her as she added, 'I'm afraid you'll just have to wait and

see what happens, but if you wait till doomsday it won't
be to see Garth and me get together.'

He leaned closer to her, his face only a short distance
from her own as his hands gripped her shoulders. 'Is
that a promise?' he demanded, his voice becoming
husky.

'Definitely. I can't stand the man.' Her pulses quickened. Was he about to kiss her, to hold her against
him? Anticipation made her nerves tingle, sending
colour to her cheeks, and in an effort to hide her inner
excitement she added, 'So you can tell Brenda she has
nothing to fear from me.'

He drew back immediately, his hands dropping from
her shoulders. It almost seemed as if her last words had
given him a vision of his friend's dark hair and flashing
dark eyes.

Linzi cursed herself for a fool, disappointment surging through her as she guessed that the mere mention
of the name had recalled him to his senses. She leaned
her head back against the pillows and closed her eyes,
then heard the bed creak as Guy stood up abruptly.

'You're tired,' he said. 'I can see you're ready to go
to sleep.'

Frustrated, she longed to shout that she was not
ready to go to sleep, but pride kept her silent. And as
she watched him carry the tray and mugs from the
room she felt an overwhelming sense of anticlimax
coupled with deep disappointment.

Previously she had feared his arrival in her room and
had wondered how she would cope with her emotions.
But when he had actually come to her he hadn't even
kissed her. Nothing had happened—nothing apart from
their usual bickering about Brenda and Garth Shaw,
which had now reached the stage of being utterly
ridiculous.

Oh, yes, there had been the odd kiss before this
evening, and he had held her in a close embrace that
had told her he longed to make love. But that had
merely been an instinctive male urge. It was not the

answer to how she could break through the depth of feeling that raised its head every time he thought of that *other woman*. Linzi writhed with jealousy as she designated Brenda to the role. Tears trickled into the pillow until emotional exhaustion sent her to sleep.

Next morning the rain was still pelting down from leaden skies, and as Linzi gazed up at the grey clouds she mumbled at them, 'You look just like I feel.' And then she discovered that her ankle felt so much better that she was able to walk without her crutches. It was enough to lift her spirits, especially when she realised how nice it was to shower without having to sit on a stool.

To celebrate the event she put on the most attractive dress she had brought with her, took extra care with her make-up, then brushed her hair until it framed her face in a mass of shining auburn waves. When she entered the kitchen she found Guy already sitting at the table. 'Look, no crutches!' she exclaimed gaily, waving empty hands in the air.

He stood up slowly, then stared at her for several long moments before he said gravely, 'You look lovely. I like you better without crutches sticking out from under your arms. They just do not suit you. And that dress sends green lights into your eyes. I suppose you know they're either more green or blue when you wear those colours?'

She felt a pleased glow. 'You've actually noticed that small point about my appearance?' she exclaimed in a voice that held amazement.

'Do you think I'm blind? I've noticed more than you imagine.' The admission came gruffly.

'Not all of which pleases you,' she returned quietly, then decided it would be wiser to veer away from the subject of herself in case it edged towards the sorrows of Brenda Shaw, or, worse still, amorous attentions of Garth Shaw. Pouring milk on her fruit and cornflakes, she asked, 'When shall we go to the museum?'

'About nine o'clock this morning. I've arranged with the person in charge to let us in before the normal opening time, which is ten a.m. That way we'll not be disturbed by people who might demand to know why you've been given permission to use a camera when such activity is not normally allowed.' The explanation came casually.

'How did you manage to do that?' she asked wonderingly.

'I've known Maggie Arrow for years. She's the mother of Robert Arrow—the friend I used to search for gold with. It's not what you know, it's whom you know.' He grinned.

A short time later rain was still falling when Guy brought the car to the back door, then held an umbrella over Linzi's head as she got into it. To keep her beneath its shelter his free arm encircled her waist in a hold that was firm enough to quicken her heartbeat and send extra colour to her cheeks. But when she sent a veiled glance towards Guy his expression was inscrutable.

Little was said as they drove over the hill where the red blossoms of the pohutukawa trees dripped with moisture, and by the time they reached the small building where the early gold-mining collection was kept the rain had stopped.

The woman who answered Guy's knock on the door was a middle-aged person with grey hair and sharp blue eyes that took in every detail of Linzi's appearance. She greeted Guy as an old friend, then demanded frankly, 'Is this your fiancée?'

He grinned but made no denial as he introduced them. 'Miss Linzi Jardine—Mrs Arrow.' Then he added, 'Thank you for coming along early to let us in, Maggie.'

The woman's eyes were still on Linzi as she said, 'If you move anything I'd be grateful if you'd put it back.'

'We'll take care to do that,' Linzi assured her. 'Thank you for allowing me to take photos.'

'Well, you have almost an hour before the door opens. Children from a school are coming, and a wet day usually brings holiday folk who haven't much to do.' She ushered them into a silent, musty room filled with relics from the past; then, gazing up at photographic enlargements on the walls, she went on, 'I wish those old faces could speak to each other. I dare say I'd learn a lot about what went on during their times.' She turned to Guy again. 'Well, I'll be in my back room when you've finished. Polaroid with instant prints, you said. I'd like to see the photos before you leave.'

'We'll show them to you, Maggie,' he said, then took Linzi's arm, drawing her towards a bench of early goldmining tools and other items relating to the district's more exciting days.

Linzi caught the gleam of interest in Maggie's eyes. It told her that Guy's action of taking her arm had not gone unnoticed by the older woman, and had confirmed her suspicion that they were more than just good friends. The thought was enough to bring a faint pinkness to her cheeks as she removed the camera from its case.

Why had he done that? she wondered. It was almost as though he'd intended to give the impression that she was somebody special to him, whereas she was anything *but* special. And, what was more, she knew she'd be wise to remember it. Nevertheless, his action had lifted her spirits. Then his voice cut further ponderings from her mind.

'That's a sluice-box,' he said, indicating a low wooden strainer-type contraption. 'Gold-bearing dirt, usually gravel from a stream, was shovelled into a dirt bucket, then poured into the top of the box to be washed and examined. You can see how it can be rocked like a cradle.'

Linzi photographed the sluice-box, then again found her arm being taken as Guy led her towards a set of scales that consisted of two round trays hanging by chains from a crossbar. His touch sent quivers along her nerves, causing her to find difficulty in holding the camera steady.

Don't be a fool—it doesn't mean a thing, she warned herself severely. It's just that he's happy to be talking about his own particular interest, the subject he's involved with at present; therefore he's in a good mood which is making him feel extra friendly. That's all it is, so don't let it go to your silly head. Bring yourself down from the clouds.

The advice continued to rumble round in Linzi's mind as they moved about the small museum, until at last she gave herself up to the enjoyment of Guy's attentions. These moments of compatability were precious, she reminded herself. They might never occur again. But despite her uplifted spirits her ankle was beginning to make itself felt again, and to rest it she sat on a square box that happened to be close at hand.

Glancing towards the door, she queried nervously, 'Do you think Mrs Arrow will mind if I sit on this box for a few minutes?'

He laughed. 'She'll mind only if your weight is too much for it. However, considering it's made of iron and is a strongbox that was used by the police for carrying the gold, it should be fairly safe from collapse.'

She felt intrigued. 'Then I'm sitting on something that has carried a fortune?' Her hands felt the hardness of the box.

'That's right, although when in use it carried the gold inside rather than on the outside,' he informed her drily.

His words amazed her, and for a moment she wondered if she'd heard them correctly, then she laughed as she said, 'You can't possibly be referring to me as *gold*. That's a complete contradiction.'

'Why not? I've heard that a good woman is worth her weight in gold.' His tone had become nonchalant.

She stared at him incredulously. 'Nor can you be referring to me as a "good woman". I doubt that you've forgotten I'm supposed to be a—husband-snatcher.'

Her eyes had filled with reproach coupled with accusation.

'If you mean that slimy fish Shaw... I'm beginning to suspect he's been tossed back into the creek.'

'Then it's a pity you can't believe he was never taken out of the creek,' Linzi retorted sharply as she stood up with an abrupt movement and made her way to another part of the museum.

After that the subject reverted to the gold-mining relics surrounding them, and while some were photographed the more simple items were rapidly sketched onto the pad that she always carried in her shoulder bag. 'I'm saving film,' she explained to Guy while applying shadow to the bottom of a round, shallow dish used for hand-panning. 'I must keep a couple of snaps for the pohutukawa tree. I've remembered about it just in time.'

This had happened near the end of her film, when, pulling her thoughts together, she'd realised that she'd completely forgotten about her own project. In some inexplicable way her mind had become engrossed with Guy's work...just as it had been taken over by the man himself. She shook herself mentally, again warning herself that to love him was hopeless, yet knowing it was impossible to stop herself from doing so.

A short time later, when they had exhausted the museum's offerings, Maggie Arrow came towards them. She glanced at the sketch-book in Linzi's hand, and at the photos Guy carried, then spoke in a firm tone. 'I'll be opening up soon, but first I always have coffee. Please come and join me.'

It sounded like an order and they followed her to the back room where she spent time during the opening hours of the museum. The photos and sketches were examined politely before the older woman betrayed the main interest hovering in her mind. However, she broached it gradually, and it soon became clear that Guy was one with whom she wished to reminisce.

'Your Coromandel friends see very little of you these days, Guy,' she said as an opening gambit.

He smiled ruefully. 'That's because I live in Auckland, Maggie.'

The older woman sighed. 'I remember your parents so well. They were a devoted couple. Your mother was a lovely woman, and your father was such a handsome man. I must say you've grown very like him in appearance.'

'Have I, Maggie? Thank you. I'm pleased about that.' A faint glimmer of pain crossed his features.

As though sensing that she was treading on tender ground, Maggie changed the subject. 'I remember how you and my Robert used to search for gold in the creeks, but you never found any, not even in that hole in the hill where there was once an open mine-shaft. Of course it's been blocked up long since those days.'

'I should hope so,' Guy said with unexpected abruptness.

Maggie continued to reminisce as her mind looked back over the years. 'And there was the girl you both had a crush on. What was her name?' She paused, frowning, trying to remember.

'Was it Brenda?' Linzi was unable to resist the question, while a sidelong glance at Guy showed his face to be expressionless.

'Yes, that's right; she was Brenda,' Maggie said brightly, then turned to Guy. 'I've often wondered if you ended up marrying her.'

'No.' The denial was almost snapped.

Maggie ignored the curtness of his tone, her attitude full of motherly interest as she went on, 'So what happened to her? I suppose she *did* marry?'

Guy's jaw tightened. 'Oh, yes. . .she married.'

Linzi sensed his reluctance to discuss the matter and her sympathy went out to him. Why on earth was the woman probing in this manner? Couldn't she see that it was a subject he had no wish to pursue? She wished someone would come into the museum and claim

Maggie's attention, but with the door still closed nobody could do so.

The older woman went on, blithely ignoring Guy's expression, which became more glum with every word she uttered. 'Well, I'm glad to know *you* didn't marry her. I'm sure it would have made your dear mother most unhappy. There was something about that girl she never liked. I know because she told me so. Your mother was always a very wise woman.' Recollection caused the grey head to nod sagely.

'Yes, I'm sure she was.' Guy replaced his mug on the bench. 'Thank you for the coffee, Maggie. We must be going.'

But Maggie hadn't finished. 'You can't leave before you've told me about your uncle Richard. I've heard he has married again. Is it true?' Her eyes gleamed as she looked at him.

'Quite true,' Guy informed her. 'In fact he has married Linzi's aunt who has lived at Coromandel for years.'

'Is that so?' Maggie's blue eyes now sparkled as they darted from one to the other. 'In that case you must feel quite close to each other. I *thought* you looked as though you were more than just *good friends*.'

Linzi spoke quickly, her colour rising as she decided that this woman was taking too much for granted. 'You are making a mistake, Mrs Arrow. Guy and I *are* just good friends. We met only recently—at the wedding.'

Maggie laughed. 'Then be warned, one wedding always brings on another,' she said teasingly.

'Well, it won't be ours,' Linzi declared firmly. 'Guy will assure you on that point.' She turned to him, expecting his concurrence, but he merely grinned at her in an irritating manner.

'So often it's the bridesmaid and best man,' Maggie said despite Linzi's words. 'Is it possible that you both stood at the altar beside your aunt and uncle?'

Guy laughed. 'Yes, we did, but I wouldn't count on

it being a sure sign. Now we really must be going home.'

'Home? May I ask where you are staying?' Maggie's question came sharply as her eyes again darted from one to the other.

'In the house of someone we both know,' Guy informed her blandly. 'Thank you for the coffee and for your help with the photos...' He paused as a sudden clamour arose outside the door.

'That'll be the schoolchildren,' Maggie said, her mouth tightening as she added, 'I hope their teacher has them under control.'

The arrival of the children proved to be a blessing that enabled them to leave without further questions being asked, and as she took her seat in the car Linzi uttered a sigh of relief, then spoke with perception. 'Mrs Arrow seemed to be full of curiosity concerning you. But she's a mother, and I suspect that in her eyes you and Robert are still little boys; therefore she has to know what mischief you've been getting into.'

He gave a short laugh. 'Do I have to remind you that I'm a big boy now? I thought you'd recognised that fact.'

'Indeed I have,' she admitted, staring straight ahead. Nor did she need reminding of the virility and charisma oozing from every pore of the man sitting beside her. Vitally aware of it, she added, 'Thank goodness you didn't go into details about our living arrangements. She'd...she'd...' She fell silent.

'Have had us in bed together?'

'It's possible,' she conceded as colour began at her neck and flooded slowly upwards.

'*Possible?* You mean it's possible for us to go to bed together? You mean you're *inviting* me? Then we must see what we can do about it. Actually... I thought you'd never ask.'

'That'll be the day,' she snapped angrily. 'You're deliberately misconstruing what I said.'

'Simmer down—I'm only joking,' he returned smoothly. 'Why must you take things so seriously?'

She made no reply. Instead she continued to stare at the road ahead, her heart filled with misery. Of course she should have realised he was only joking, but how could he be so flippant about something that, to her, would be so precious?

Little was said as they drove through the town, although Guy sent several swift glances towards Linzi. 'You're looking very pensive,' he said at last. 'Almost sad, in fact. I can hardly believe that my facetious remark was enough to make your lip quiver and your eyes moist.'

She blinked rapidly while pulling herself together, then tossed off a shaky laugh. 'I am not about to weep over anything,' she assured him, making an effort to convince even herself of this fact. Then, raking about in her mind for a topic of conversation, she said, 'I was interested in hearing about the mine-shaft Mrs Arrow mentioned. It reminded me of the hole near the cottage, or perhaps it could be called a cave.'

Surprised, he raised his dark brows. 'What hole near the cottage? I presume you mean Kauri Cottage?'

'Of course. It's in one of the steep hillsides towards the back of the cottage, less than ten minutes' walk away. It's not a shaft, nor does it go very far into the hill, but Aunt Bea thinks that at one time somebody dug there in a search for gold.'

Guy nodded. 'It's more than likely. There was a time when numerous holes were being dug on the Coromandel Peninsula. Everyone was hopeful of finding gold. I'd like to see this particular hole.'

'It's not easy to find. There is no obvious track to it, and over the years the opening has become concealed by manuka scrub.'

'But you know where it is?' He sent her a sharp glance.

'Oh, yes, I can find it.'

His voice became eager. 'Then you'll take me there as soon as we get home.'

She bristled. 'That sounds more like an order than a request. Not even a *please* attached to it.' She paused thoughtfully then queried, 'Is it possible that in return you'll take me to see the shaft Mrs Arrow mentioned?'

He frowned, then said evasively, 'There'll be nothing to see. You heard her say it has been blocked up.'

'Still, I'd like to see the place where it is,' she persisted, suddenly gripped by a strong desire to be shown one of his boyhood haunts. In time to come it would be something to remember.

'It's too wet,' he demurred. 'Have you forgotten the rain?'

She laughed. 'You *know* it's stopped raining. You've even turned your windscreen wipers off. Besides, you didn't consider it too wet to go to the hole in the hill.'

'That'll be different,' he argued stubbornly. 'The shaft is fronted by a bush area where leaf-mould will make it messy underfoot.'

'That won't matter. We're both wearing heavy shoes,' she pointed out with quiet determination. 'We're also wearing raincoats.'

'So that when we get home there'll be no need to take them off. You can lead me straight to the hole, or the cave. . .or whatever.'

Glancing at him, she noticed that his frown had deepened. Her lips compressed into a firm line as she said, 'I'll do that after you've shown me the shaft where you and Robert searched for gold. No shaft, no hole.'

He remained silent, his expression grim.

Puzzled, she went on, 'Why do I get the feeling you're reluctant to show me it? I can't see that it's any big hassle, unless. . . Ah, I think I can guess: you *didn't* go there with Robert—it was one of your haunts with Brenda.'

'You're quite wrong,' he snapped with sudden impatience. 'Brenda never went there with us. Nor can I understand your determination to see this place.'

'Just as I can't understand your reluctance to show it to me. OK, as I said before—no shaft, no hole,' she said, and a deep sigh betrayed her intense disappointment.

There was a short silence while he thought about it, then, unexpectedly, he changed his mind. His voice gruff, he said, 'Very well, we'll go there now. You may take a quick look and that's all.'

'Thank you, Guy,' she said quietly, her face relaxing into a happier expression. 'I really do want to see it.'

The decision made, the car leapt forward, taking them beyond the town to where the road turned towards the range of mountains dividing the long, narrow peninsula. For a short distance they remained on flat ground bordered by residential houses, then they rose abruptly to twist and turn between bush-clad slopes.

'We used to ride here on our bikes,' he said briefly.

'*Bikes?* How far is it?' Linzi gasped while visualising the two boys pushing their way uphill on a gravel road.

'Only about a mile. We're here now.' Guy stopped the car on the wide, grassy verge of a road corner. 'How does your ankle feel? Do you think it'll take you a short distance over wet, mushy ground?'

'Of course.' She had no intention of allowing the ache in her ankle to stand in the way.

'OK, but watch your step for protruding tree roots. I'll lead the way. There used to be a track, but I dare say it's overgrown.'

They left the car, and Linzi found herself trailing behind Guy, who pushed his way amongst tall trees and the shrubbery growing between their trunks. Progress was slow, impeded by a growth of ferns underfoot that swept her legs and the dripping branches of bushes that brushed her face. It was also necessary to guard her ankle while stepping over roots, but despite the discomfort she knew that whatever the circumstances she would follow this man wherever he went.

After a short distance they came to an area where

the hillside flattened out into a wide shelf at the base of a cliff. In one place there was a large, creeper-covered mound that looked as if it had been formed by a fall of rock from above. Guy moved towards it.

'It used to be here,' he said. 'If you push away the creepers you'll find a heap of rubble. As Maggie said, the opening has been blocked. Does it satisfy you, or must I clear the rubble so that you can actually see it?' His tone held a sardonic ring.

'No. . .of course not,' she faltered.

'That's a relief. I'm sure you'll agree that it's better for a dead mine to remain hidden. Did you know that the entrance to a mine is known as an adit?'

'I noticed the word in your manuscript.' She was feeling guilty about her determination to see this place, which had turned out to be something of an anticlimax. To hide her disappointment she turned to gaze up into the nearby lofty trees, then inhaled deep breaths of the subtle aroma caused by bush dampness and leaf-mould. Then, feeling that something was expected of her, she asked, 'How long ago is it since you were here?'

'Not since that ghastly day—' He stopped suddenly and turned away as an expression of anguish crossed his face.

Puzzled, she stared at his back, aware that her simple question had caused him pain. Instinctively, she knew that something had happened the last time he'd been here—something that had made him reluctant to return. Speaking quietly, she said, 'Guy. . . I know you didn't want to come here. Was it because of Brenda? Is this where she rejected you in favour of Garth Shaw?'

He swung round to look at her, his eyes till bleak. 'Have you forgotten I told you I did *not* bring Brenda to this particular place?'

'No. . .but I can't help feeling. . .'

'That I *lied* to you? Is that it? You're accusing me of being a *liar*, which is something I hate. Thank you very much.'

She faced his anger calmly. 'I felt that only Brenda could have made you feel so—so upset about this place. Won't you tell me about it? You know all that business about a trouble shared being a trouble halved.'

He looked at her in silence for several moments, then, as if her sympathy had reached out to touch him, he spoke gruffly. 'OK, I'll tell you about it. . .'

CHAPTER EIGHT

GUY raised his head and squared his broad shoulders. His voice low and almost apologetic, he said, 'If you'll ignore my black mood I'll try to shake it off. It's just that I'm gripped by bitter memories—memories I feared might drag me back to a certain day if I came here.'

'They have done just that?' she queried, feeling guilty because of her own part in this dragging-back.

He went on, 'My last visit to this place was on a day when one part of my life ended and another part of it began. I remember it was a Saturday afternoon. It was a day when I learnt that the unexpected can raise its head and alter one's entire existence.' He paused to look at her thoughtfully. 'Have you ever noticed how you can plan your day, and then something unexpected happens to change everything?'

'Yes, I've noticed. . .but please go on.'

'Robert and I looked upon this as our secret place. We came here with candles and small tools to scratch at the walls of the shaft, hoping to find gold that had been missed by the experts of earlier days. I think we expected to find it blinking at us in the candlelight, and as we chipped away we planned what we'd do with the wealth.'

Linzi's eyes widened with concern. 'Wasn't it dangerous to go into the shaft?'

'We didn't go far because we were too scared to venture more than a few yards from the adit. Anyway, on this particular Saturday an argument developed, and this was followed by a fight outside the shaft, right here on this open area.'

'What was it about?' She was unable to resist the question.

There was a momentary silence before he admitted with reluctance, 'It was over Brenda. Robert had made derogatory remarks about her behaviour with some of the other boys. I gave him a split lip, a black eye and a bleeding nose. His face was covered in blood when he rushed away to grab his bike and ride down the hill.'

'Leaving you full of remorse, I suppose,' she said with understanding, at the same time feeling that there was more to come.

'You can say that again! For a long time I sat huddled like a hulk of misery. We had never fought before, and I knew that our friendship of years was at an end. However, when Robert reached his home my uncle was there searching for me. He was told where I could be found.

'Uncle came roaring up the hill in his car, and discovered me nursing the blows Robert had delivered. But they were nothing to the blow he was about to deliver. It was the news that both my parents had been killed in a car accident.'

A hand flew to her mouth as a gasp escaped her. Tears sprang to her eyes while her heart felt ready to burst with an overflow of sympathy; then, unable to control the impulse, her arms reached out to embrace him. It was a gesture of compassion with which she tried to offer comfort, and, in doing so, she pressed her head against his shoulder.

His arms held her against him in a firm clasp, and although he made no attempt to kiss her they stood together in silence while tears rolled down her cheeks. 'Richard and I stood just like this,' he murmured above her head. 'We both wept.'

Linzi made an effort to stifle a sob, but it shook her slim form.

'I didn't mean to upset you, to make you feel like this.' Guy released her gently, then fished in his pocket for a clean handkerchief. 'Here. . .take this. It'll work better than any lacy wisp you'll have with you.'

'Thank you.' She blew her nose and mopped the

tears. 'Now I know why you had no wish to come here. Let's get away from the place.'

He said, 'To be honest, I decided to put myself to the test, but I'm afraid it all came crowding back. This will always be a haunted place for me—a place signifying the end of my parents as well as the end of a schoolboy friendship.'

Linzi glanced at her watch. 'It's time we had lunch,' she said with decision. 'There's nothing like food to lay ghosts.'

'Good idea. We'll eat in town and wash them away with a glass of wine.' He looked at her intently. 'Do you know you're a great little pal, or is that something I forgot to mention?'

For a moment her spirits rose, then sank almost immediately. 'A great little pal'. It was not what she had in mind as far as Guy was concerned, and she seethed with frustration as she followed him back to the car.

Little was said as they drove down the hill, and by the time they were sitting in the restaurant Linzi was thankful to see that he appeared to have put aside his sad memories. The photos taken in the museum were a help in achieving this—these, along with her own sketches, were examined while they sipped the wine that complemented their seafood lunch.

Later, when they returned to Kauri Cottage, she settled herself on the lounge settee where she was able to sit with her foot up. She knew she had used it more than was good for it, and could only hope that its aching would subside.

Across her lap was a tray that tilted, while on a small table beside her were pencils, pens, black drawing ink and a block of heavy quality cartridge paper. The photos and sketches were also there, and as she examined each one she wondered where to begin.

She knew that Guy was working on his manuscript in the dining room, and because she could hear the faint sound of his word processor she also knew that he had not shut the door. She was glad about that because she hated it when he shut the door. It made her feel shut out and as though he'd put a barrier between them, pushing their relationship right back to when he'd been so angered by her arrival. In fact, even further back—to the wedding, when he'd first listened to Brenda's lies about her and Garth.

Did he still believe Brenda to be Madam Truth personified? Of course he did. He'd had no reason to change his mind about *that*. What on earth had the woman said to him over the phone? Linzi would have given much to have heard Brenda's side of those conversations.

'Snap out of it and get on with the job,' she muttered to herself with a sudden burst of irritation. Then, using a pencil, she began to copy one of her museum sketches onto the better quality cartridge paper. When it was finished she went over the lines with a pen and black ink, then studied it critically. It would reproduce well, she thought with satisfaction, hoping that Guy would be pleased.

She worked steadily until the end of the afternoon, and by that time she had several pen-and-ink sketches ready to show him. Also by that time she had wearied of drawing such mundane items, and, placing them in a neat heap on the table, she allowed her imagination to run free with a series of humorous dream sketches.

In them a miner lay in his camp-bed, blissfully dreaming of a gold nugget that was too heavy to lift... a pile of nuggets that broke the scales...a sack of gold being literally dragged into the bank. And as the ideas flowed she sketched rapidly in pencil until she had six cartoon-type drawings that made her laugh.

But suddenly the thought that Guy might not find them amusing made her pause to wonder if he'd consider her to be treating his serious work in a facetious manner. The fear was enough to make her conceal them at the back of her sketch-pad, and in any case it was time to stop and prepare the evening meal.

However, the enjoyment of doing the cartoons had lifted her spirits, and as she moved about the kitchen more ideas entered her head, bringing a smile to her lips. Later, while watching Guy cut into a tender steak, she pondered the question of telling him about them, but again she feared he might think that they lowered the dignity of his work.

Next morning the heavy rainclouds had vanished, leaving the sun to shine from a clear sky that threw blue brilliance into the sea. A light southerly breeze stirred the crisp, clean air, and as Linzi stood on the front veranda to inhale its freshness it lifted the auburn tendrils framing her face.

Guy came to stand beside her, the tang of his aftershave causing her to take an even deeper breath. And as she turned to look at him she wondered if she would ever get the memory of his handsome face, his well-built form and his vitality out of her mind. His dark hair held the groomed sheen of a black shag perched on a rock near the beach, and his hazel eyes held a question as they met her own, which now reflected the colour of the sea.

'You have a plan for today?' he queried.

'Of course—I'll be working as usual.'

'No doubt, but working at what? Surely the painting of the cottage is finished? Another brush stroke will ruin it.'

'I'll decide upon that after I've lived with it for a while. One usually sees a little something that needs to be done at a later date. In the meantime I'll begin work on those twisted branches and grey-green foliage of the pohutukawa tree. The background areas of sea and sky are sufficiently dry.' She paused, then asked, 'Why are you interested in my plan for today?'

His eyes rested upon the softness of her sweetly generous mouth as he said, 'I'm wondering if it includes keeping the promise you made—the one about showing me where to find the hole in the hillside. You declared you'd do so only if I showed you the shaft, remember?'

'Yes, I'm sorry about that. I had no right to keep on about going there when I knew you had no wish to do so.' Linzi felt guilty all over again, knowing that her persistence had caused him pain.

'Well, I kept my side of the bargain. Shall we go after lunch? We'll both be ready for a break by then. Do you think your ankle will stand the walk?'

'Yes, it's not troubling me at all this morning.'

'Good.' He turned and stared at the tree which stood slightly left of them between the cottage and the beach. The trunk leaned over as it rose above roots protruding from the gravel and sandy soil, and the clusters of red blossoms, brilliant in the morning sun, gave an atmosphere of warm festivity.

'The New Zealand Christmas tree,' Guy murmured. 'There's something unforgettable about a pohutukawa in full bloom. From where shall you paint it?'

She gave a small laugh. 'I changed my mind about that at least three times before the obvious answer struck me. I've now decided to do the view of it from Aunt Bea's bedroom window. It's the one that she knows best—the one that she saw first when she opened the curtains each morning.'

'You have a similar view from this veranda,' he pointed out.

'Yes, but this light breeze is sure to become stronger, and that will be a nuisance, whereas in the bedroom I'll be sheltered from it,' she explained.

'You're right. I'll help you get set up.'

'Thank you, but there's no need. I can manage.'

He ignored her protest by striding into the third bedroom. Her easel was moved into the front room she was using, and it was followed by her painting equipment and stool.

Linzi hastened to spread newspaper to protect the carpet from any accidentally dropped brushes or tubes of paint. And then she became aware of Guy's keen interest as she squeezed daubs of colour round the edge of her palette.

'You look really professional,' he said. 'I can see you've done it before.'

'Do I detect a hint of amusement. . .?'

'Of course not. To be honest I'd like to stay and watch you at work, but you've already told me it disturbs you.'

'Yes, I'm afraid it does,' she admitted, then added to herself, But not in the way you think. His presence, she realised, was becoming increasingly disturbing to her emotions, and she was beginning to wonder how to cope with the sudden sensations of desire that sprang to life whenever he was near. To soften the dismissal she said, 'I usually make a mess when people watch me at work.'

He spoke drily. 'That's as good as telling me to get the hell out of it—back to my own work, in fact.'

Linzi remained calm. 'I understood you to be the one who feared disturbance to the work project. I've done enough of that already, and now I seem to be doing it again, but in a different way.'

He spoke fiercely. 'You're dead right—you have disturbed my work. You've thrown it completely out of gear—in more ways than one.'

His tone took her by surprise, causing her to look at him with dismay. 'More ways. . .? What do you mean?'

'You know damned well what I mean. You've caused hassles I can do without, to say nothing of mental distractions I don't need.' Irritation caused his chin to jut at her.

'Then why don't you try to forget them?' she retorted sharply.

'I wish I could,' he snapped, then strode from the room.

His departure was a relief that enabled her to begin concentrating, although at first her hand was unsteady as she placed umber branches in position. However, within a short time her tension left her as the tree, with its light and dark patches of foliage, began to take shape on the canvas.

Time sped by, and at noon she left the easel to prepare a lunch of scrambled eggs made tasty by the addition of bacon. Was Guy still seething with irritation? she wondered, then felt reassured when he grinned at her across the kitchen table.

'Are you ready for your walk to the hole in the hill?' he queried.

She nodded. 'I'll enjoy the fresh air. I'm afraid the smell of turps and linseed oil is all through the house. I'm sorry about that,' she apologised, feeling guilty because this was something else he was forced to endure on her account.

His broad shoulders lifted in a slight shrug. 'It doesn't worry me. It's a clean, tangy type of odour. In fact I rather like it.'

'It's a studio smell that I live with.' She smiled. 'You wouldn't wish to—no, of course you wouldn't.'

'I can think of worse things,' he returned enigmatically.

'Such as?'

'Such as not being able to smell anything at all.'

Later they pushed their way through long grass towards the steep hill that rose a short distance from the back of the cottage. It presented a bleak face of bare patches that were broken by areas of rock, and scrubby growth that clung precariously.

Guy stood still to send a sweeping glance over the area. 'Not an attractive place,' he commented.

Linzi followed his gaze towards the heights. 'I can see colours in it. There's red and purple and a coppery shade. There's yellow and something that looks quite goldish. Do you think it could be gold?'

Guy laughed. 'I doubt it. It's more likely to be iron pyrites—a gold-coloured iron which can be mistaken for gold. It's known as fool's gold, and will be the reason why somebody started digging this hole we're about to see. Many of the early prospectors had their hopes dashed by fool's gold.'

When they reached the hole there was little to see apart from the fact that it receded into the hill to form a large cave. The roof and walls appeared to be solid but the floor, lying below the level of the entrance, was covered with water from the recent rains. The stone Guy threw into it fell with a dull, echoing plop, causing him to remark, 'When the water drains away it will leave a floor that's too deep in mud to walk across.'

Linzi perched herself on a nearby rock then said in an apologetic tone, 'You're probably finding this an anticlimax. It's not as interesting as the shaft on the hill road—' She stopped abruptly, annoyed with herself for having mentioned the place that held such sadness for him; but, watching him anxiously, she was relieved to see that he did not appear to be unduly perturbed.

Instead, he surprised her by coming closer to take her hands and draw her to her feet. Looking down into her face, he spoke in a low voice. 'At least I now have something pleasant to remember about that place.'

'Oh?' She stared up into his eyes, trying to fathom their expression, and for some inexplicable reason her heart began to beat a little faster—not that it ever did anything else when he touched her.

He went on, his voice still low, 'I shall always remember the look of deep compassion on your face, the tears of sympathy you shed on my account. Thank you for that understanding; it will never be forgotten.'

'I—I just wanted to comfort you. . .'

'You did, especially when you put your arms around me. Would you care to repeat the exercise?' Unexpectedly he drew her against him, as he lowered his head, his lips found hers.

It was a long, tender kiss that filled her with hope. Was it possible that he loved her? The question drummed in her mind in time to the beat of her heart, and with a sense of happy anticipation she waited for the words she longed to hear.

But they did not come, even though his lips trailed across her brow and closed lids—even though they slid down her cheeks and came to rest once more on her mouth, this time with passion.

Patience, she told herself, responding with an ardour she was unable to control. At least he's not as allergic to me as I imagined, despite the interruptions to his work. The thought caused her arms to tighten about his neck and her fingers to fondle the dark hair at his nape.

A small groan escaped him as he clasped her against the length of his vibrant body, the intimate pressure telling her of the desire raging within him. And as his lips went to a vulnerable pulse in her neck his hand moved to hold her breast, his thumb gently stroking the nipple that had become as taut as an unopened rosebud.

The delicious sensations racing through her body clawed at her stomach, filling her with complete help-lessness against the onslaught of her longing to give herself to this man here and now. Her love for him made her response to his call even more uninhibited, causing an involuntary arch against him, and dragging a groan from his lips.

But suddenly, after another passionate kiss, Guy had himself under control. His hands went to her shoulders as he stepped back to stare down into her rosy, upturned face. His voice husky with emotion, he said, 'Conditions will not allow me to do my caveman stuff.'

She blinked at him. 'Caveman stuff. . .?'

'Yes. Here is the woman, there is the cave, but the floor is unsuitable to drag her by the hair in the acknowledged fashion.'

An icy coldness crept over her, chilling her spirits to freezing point as she got the message. He was making light of those precious moments that had carried her up into the heavens. He was telling her in this facetious manner that they didn't mean a thing. . .at least, not to him. And, knowing what they meant to her, she was left with a sense of shock that dragged her back to earth.

Pride made her force a smile, and, struggling to sound casual rather than bitter, she said, 'I understand perfectly. I suppose most males are cavemen at heart. Their egos demand conquest. They must display their sexual prowess and then move on to the next triumph. Actually. . .you remind me of Garth Shaw.'

He took a deep, hissing breath as his expression became thunderous. 'Are you daring to compare me to *him*? What's brought on such a damned insult?'

'The fact that I see very little difference between you.' She spun round and began to make her way back to the cottage before tears sprang into her eyes. At the same time she cursed herself. *Idiot*, her common sense told her fiercely. *Idiot*. To allow yourself to get so carried away. Let that be a warning. His sexual appetite needs satisfying. . .and that's all it is. As for him feeling any real love for *you*. . .you can forget it. His mind is completely wrapped up in Brenda because he's one of those rare types—*a one-woman man*.

The thoughts flung themselves about in Linzi's mind, and by the time she reached the cottage the tears were flowing freely. Her spirits had been dragged down to a state of depression that made her long to pack her bag and leave for home there and then. However, the tangy aroma of linseed and turps was enough to switch her thoughts to the tasks waiting to be done, and instead of pulling her suitcase from beneath the bed she went to the bathroom where she tried to remove the ravages of her tears by pressing a cold, wet flannel to her eyes.

After that she returned to the bedroom, where she stared unseeingly through the front window until her attention was caught by the sight of Guy leaving the drive. He's taking a walk, she thought, and watched as he strode towards the first corner of the road.

On reaching it, he paused, then turned and retraced his steps, and even from that distance she could see that his head was bowed, as though he was deep in unhappy thoughts. He was thinking about Brenda, she decided—Brenda, whose words he believed implicitly because he was so positive she'd never lie to him.

And it was then that Linzi realised that they were both in similar situations. They both loved someone who was out of bounds. Sympathy caused her heart to reach out to him, but she knew that to offer further comfort was beyond her. Sighing, she returned to her easel, and a short time later the faint sound of the word processor told her that he was again at work in the dining room.

By four o'clock she felt ready for a cup of coffee, so she went to the kitchen, boiled the kettle and made it in the cafetière. When it was poured she carried her own mug and one for Guy into the dining room, placing his on the table beside him.

He looked at her with gratitude. 'Thank you, I'm more than ready for coffee. Does this mean you've got over your tantrum because I kissed you?'

She sent him a cool stare. '*Tantrum?* What are you talking about?'

'As if you didn't know.' He snorted. 'I'm referring to that recent bout of fury. Was it because you feared caveman tactics? Really, I was only joking.'

'I'm sure you were—and for your information that wasn't a tantrum. It was a reaction to—to something else that thoroughly upset me.. something you wouldn't understand.'

He frowned as though trying to recall what that could have been, until at last he said, 'Tell me and I'll try to make amends.'

She shook her head. 'Certainly not. I have no intention of discussing it.' How could she explain that she was upset because those moments which had meant so much to her had obviously meant so little to him? It would betray her love for him, and that must be avoided at all costs.

Sipping his coffee, he watched her over the rim of his mug, his hazel eyes thoughtful as they studied her face. At last he said, 'I think you should tell me. It would clear the air.'

Again she shook her head. 'The air will clear itself. It usually does. I suppose we all experience things that upset us, but sooner or later we get over them to a certain extent.'

'You're right, but that doesn't mean we forget them.'

She saw sadness creep into his eyes and guessed that the tragedy of his parents' death had sprung into his mind. In an effort to take his thoughts from it she searched for any other reason why he might be feeling such misery, but knew of only one; therefore she said gently, 'It must have upset you greatly to sit in the church and watch Brenda get married, but time is a great healer.'

'Is it indeed?' His mouth twisted as he spoke drily. 'Well, it might interest you to learn that I didn't sit in a church and watch Brenda get married.'

His words surprised her. 'You mean. . .you weren't invited?'

'At the time I was in the South Island gathering material for one of my books. I was away for several weeks, and when I came home I was told she was married.' He gave a slight shrug, as though to brush the subject aside.

'Oh. . .well. . .it was better for you to have missed it,' Linzi said in a sympathetic voice, thinking of the heartbreak it would have caused him.

Guy gave a mirthless grin. 'I wasn't the only person to be absent. Even her parents missed it.'

'You mean they were also away?'

'No. I mean it wasn't a normal sort of wedding that takes place in a church or garden setting. I was told it was a register-office affair that takes only a few minutes.'

Linzi felt a sudden sympathy for Brenda. 'How sad,' she said quietly. 'Most girls long to be a bride in a church wedding, with a bridal gown and all the trimmings, but this sounds more like an elopement. I wonder why they did it that way?'

'Because her parents didn't approve of her choice... or so I was told.' Guy drained his coffee before he went on, 'I suppose the situation began when Brenda became disenchanted with living in this small town of Coromandel. She yearned for the bright lights of a larger place, so found herself a job in Thames.'

'Where she also found Garth Shaw,' Linzi said with perception.

'Exactly. He had established a picture-framing business, and had a home of his own. Apparently she moved in with him. Naturally, she took him to Coromandel to meet her parents, but they did not approve of him. They were also upset because she was living with him, and did their best to persuade her to leave him. This happened on every visit they made, until on one occasion they told her parents that they loved each other...and that they'd been to the register office and were now married.' Guy lapsed into silence.

'Brenda told you all this?' Linzi asked.

'No, her parents told me. Needless to say, they were not amused but had to make the best of it.'

'Just as you have had to make the best of it,' Linzi said in a dull tone, thinking that she herself would have to do likewise.

Guy's only reply was to return his attention to the word processor, hinting that the subject was closed.

But Linzi had a last word. 'Poor Brenda,' she said on leaving the room. 'She will now know the truth of Mother knowing best.'

When she returned to her easel she found that the scene outside had changed. The sunlight was now falling on the subject from a slightly different angle, changing the light and darker areas of the tree and making it necessary to work from the Polaroid photo she'd taken earlier. She held it in her hand to study it carefully, and was so engrossed that she failed to realise a car had stopped outside until its door banged.

Startled, she glanced out of the window, but as she was unable to see a car she realised that it must be in their driveway. Moments later there were footsteps on the veranda. They paused at the open front door, and then Linzi froze at the sound of a feminine voice.

'Guy. . . Are you there, Guy? *Guy*, where are you?'

Brenda had arrived.

Linzi sat as though turned to cold stone, mainly because she felt unable to move. Guy could deal with this, she decided. He was the one Brenda had come to see, and it was with relief that she heard him go to the door. She also heard his voice echo his surprise.

'Good grief. . . Brenda. . .what the hell are you doing here?'

'I had to come. I must talk to you. I don't get any satisfaction over the phone because you seem so remote.' Brenda's voice was full of pathos. 'Aren't you going to ask me in?'

'Not until I know why you're here. Nor can I see what I can do.'

'You can at least *listen* to me. You can *advise* and tell me what to do, just as you always did. Guy. . . *dear*. . .you were always such a friend—such a *close* friend. . .'

'That ended when you married Shaw. You've got him to advise you now, so why come to me?' Guy's voice was cutting.

'Him? Huh—*him*!' Brenda's voice was full of scorn. 'There's a lot I want to explain about him. Guy, I made a mistake. I want to tell you about it.'

'I'm not sure that I want to hear about it.'

'But you must listen about Garth and—and *her*!' Brenda exclaimed.

'Who do you mean by *her*?' Guy rasped.

Linzi was surprised by the sudden coldness in his tone. She had remained crouched on her stool, almost paralysed from the shock of Brenda's arrival, and, while she knew she was eavesdropping, she also knew that their conversation would concern herself.

This proved to be a fact when Brenda went on,' Who do I mean? You *know* who I mean. It's that—that *Linzi* woman, of course—that stupid twit who imagines she's an *artist*. I wouldn't hang one of her daubs in the toilet.' The words were uttered furiously.

'So what about your husband and. . .her?' Guy drawled.

'He's gone away with her, that's what,' Brenda spat. 'I told you about it on the phone but you didn't seem to believe me, so I've come to convince you—and to be comforted. Guy. . .*dear*. . .you will comfort me?' The last words came as a whine.

'Well, I'll admit it was rather difficult to believe you.'

'Why? You know I always tell you the truth,' Brenda maintained.

Listening, Linzi gasped at the audacity of those words, although even she was becoming fascinated by Brenda's story. Fortunately, the latter was unable to see her because the bedroom door was partly closed, otherwise the story would not have continued.

'There's another reason I'm here,' Brenda said. 'I've come to tell you that Garth and I are finished. I can't take him back after seeing her in his arms,' she said pathetically.

'When did this happen?' Guy demanded.

'Three days ago. I followed him to her parents' home. She opened the door and I saw them embrace and kiss each other. She's living there alone at present, so you can guess what happened next. It's what made me long to run to you for comfort. I thought that perhaps you and I. . .' Her words trailed away.

'Yes? You and I could what?' he demanded curtly.

'Well. . .get together. I know you had a crush on me at school.'

'That was years ago when I was a callow youth. I see things differently now.' His voice was noncommittal.

Linzi had listened anxiously for Guy's response to the suggestion that they should get together. So far she had heard no sign of great joy engendered by Brenda's arrival, and she began to wonder if she had been mistaken in assuming that he loved her. And then his voice came to her ears again.

'You said they've gone away together. What makes you so sure about that, Brenda?'

'Because I saw her come out of the house and get into his car. She carried a suitcase. Wherever they are they'll be sleeping together, I know they will,' Brenda declared vehemently.

Linzi clapped a hand to her mouth while fighting the urge to rush out and confront Brenda, and then Guy's next words caused her to remain on the stool.

His voice held a hint of amusement as he drawled, 'When did this optical illusion take place?'

'The day before yesterday—and it wasn't an optical illusion. They didn't see me because they were too wrapped up in each other. It's just as I told you on the phone, so why can't you believe me?' Brenda's voice was full of frustration.

'Because I'm sure you've made a mistake,' Guy said in a weary tone. 'Perhaps it was somebody who looked like Linzi.'

Brenda's voice rose to an angry pitch. 'It wasn't a mistake. It was *her*. Don't you think I know what *she* looks like?' she ranted furiously.

Guy ignored the question as he drawled in a voice that dripped with sarcasm, 'This happened—*when* did you say?'

'I *told* you, it was the day before yesterday,' she repeated.

'I think you're lying.' The accusation came coldly.

'No, Guy, dear; I'd *never* lie to you. I *feel* for you too much. Why don't you ask me inside? I've brought a suitcase.'

'You intend to stay here...*with us*?' His words echoed his surprise.

'Of course. Didn't I say I've finished with Garth?' She paused, then gave a loud sniff. 'What's the smell that's in this house? It hit me as I came to the door.'

Linzi felt she'd heard enough. The thought of Brenda staying in the cottage with them gave her the horrors; therefore she sprang up from the stool and swept out into the passage in time to answer the question.

In a cool voice she said, 'The smell, Brenda, is a mixture of linseed oil and turps. It's a medium I use with my oil paints. Guy is becoming quite accustomed to it,' she added casually.

CHAPTER NINE

BRENDA was visibly shaken by the sight of Linzi. Her face went scarlet, then lost its colour to a deathly pallor. Her eyes widened into black orbs and her jaw sagged as she croaked, 'Wh-what are you doing here?'

'Just painting and sketching,' Linzi told her. 'I've been here for almost a week. I can show you the work to prove it.'

Brenda's face jerked towards Guy. 'Is this true?' she demanded furiously, her chest heaving with agitation.

'Perfectly true,' he admitted in a dry tone. 'Now you know why I found such difficulty in believing your story. While you claimed Linzi was with your husband I knew she was here with me.'

Linzi spoke earnestly. 'Please believe me, Brenda, I have never encouraged Garth away from you. As far as I'm concerned, he's all yours. I feel sure he loves you,' she added lamely.

Brenda ignored her. Her hand shook slightly as she brushed her dark hair from her face, and, speaking directly to Guy, she said, 'Am I to understand that—that you and *she* have been living together in this house for almost a week?'

He nodded. 'I'm unable to deny it—although it's more like four days. . .'

Brenda's face became red with anger as she drew in a long, hissing breath. 'That means you're sleeping together—'

'It does not,' he cut in. 'If you look through the house you'll see that we have our own bedrooms. In any case, I'm at a loss to know what the hell our sleeping arrangements have to do with you.' The last words were gritted at her.

'It seems clear enough to me,' Linzi put in.

'You shut up,' Brenda snapped at her fiercely.

Unperturbed, Linzi continued to speak to Guy. Her voice well modulated, she said, 'You must understand it's a shock for Brenda to find me here—especially as she hopes to move in with you.'

Guy's brows shot up.

'That's why she has brought a suitcase,' Linzi said, forcing a smile to hide her own growing agitation.

'*Two* suitcases,' Brenda amended. She looked at Guy anxiously. 'You *do* want me, don't you, Guy, dear? I have a strong feeling you've *always* wanted me, so please tell me,' she added pathetically.

He merely stared at her in silence.

Linzi studied his face, trying to read his thoughts, but his expression was unfathomable. Cautiously she said, 'Brenda has already told you she is finished with Garth. If she moves in with you she has only to wait for two years and the marriage will be over even without having to use my name as the cause of the breakup.' It was a desperate attempt to warn him of impending danger—unless, of course, this was a situation he'd be happy to accept.

Guy scowled at Brenda. 'Is this true? Is this what you have in mind? You're definitely leaving Shaw?'

Brenda sent him a dazzling smile. 'Haven't I said so? And what's more I'm tired of standing in this doorway.' She pushed past Linzi and made her way into the lounge where she stood examining the furniture. 'Well, this is OK, I suppose. I'll be happy here.'

'That's if you stay here,' Linzi said pointedly, then looked at Guy, waiting for him to resolve this question.

Before he could speak Brenda sent her a baleful glare then spoke to Guy in a pleading tone. 'Can't we talk in private. . .away from her flapping ears?'

Guy's tone became sardonic. 'I suspect Linzi is finding this as good as a soap opera. However, I'd like to get this straight. You say you're leaving Shaw, but so far I have not heard the word "divorce" mentioned in connection with your husband.'

Brenda's voice rose to a higher pitch. 'You can stop referring to him as my *husband. I haven't got a husband*—' She broke off suddenly.

Guy's brows became a black bar. 'What the hell are you talking about? How else can I refer to him?'

'You can call him my *partner*,' Brenda admitted sulkily, then bit her lower lip before going on nervously, 'We're. . .well, as it happens we're not actually married. . .'

'*What?*' Guy stared at her in amazement.

Brenda rushed on, 'Please try to understand the situation. You see, it was like this. We began by living together to make sure we were suitable for each other, but you know how old-fashioned Mummy and Daddy are. They became agitated because we were living in what they called "sin", so on one of our visits we told them we'd been to the register office and got married. It didn't take long for me to become known as Brenda Shaw.'

'But legally you're still Brenda Browne,' Guy mused. 'I'll admit this is something of a shock. So. . .where is Shaw now?'

'I told you, he's gone away with—' She pulled herself up just in time, and added hastily, 'I—I must've been mistaken about seeing *her* get into his car.'

'Then it's time you visited an optometrist,' Guy snapped. 'And there's something else you'd better know: if you tell me any more lies I'll rip strips off you.'

The smile Brenda sent him was beguiling. 'That means you'll forgive me for any that I *have* told. Guy, darling, I *knew* you would.' And then a subtle change in her manner indicated a more dominant attitude as she went on, 'My cases are in the car. If you wouldn't mind bringing them in. . . And then you may show me where I'm to sleep. Actually, I rather fancy the front room.' She smiled at him hopefully.

The word sent a shock of horror through Linzi. Her jaw dropped a fraction. She was shaken by the thought

of Brenda staying with them, and, pulling herself
together, she snapped furiously, 'You shall not occupy
any room. My aunt owns this cottage and I'm here at
her request. That makes me the hostess in this place. I
have *not* invited you to stay, nor have I any intention
of doing so, unless—unless Guy particularly wishes you
to stay,' she finished lamely as this ghastly thought
struck her.

Guy made no reply. He had moved to the window
and now stood with his back to them, staring through
the glass pane as though deep in thought.

Watching him, Linzi wondered if he'd heard a word
she'd said, then she turned to Brenda to offer her some
advice. 'If you're wise you'll return to Thames and be
there to greet Garth when he comes home.'

'I doubt that he'll do that,' Brenda said with a hint
of pathos in her voice. 'I—I feel he's deserted me.'

'Is that because you've made his life unbearable with
your constant nagging?' Linzi demanded with sudden
insight.

'Well, there have been times when he'd needed a
jolly good telling-off,' Brenda admitted sulkily.

Linzi could believe her, but spoke quietly as she
made a suggestion. 'Why not try changing your tactics?
Why not try a little loving?'

'I don't need your advice,' Brenda snapped at her
fiercely. 'I know what I'm doing. I've come here to be
with Guy. . .and I'll stay here whether you like it or
not. He *wants* me to stay—I *know* he does.'

Linzi crossed the room to where Guy stood at the
window, his back still turned towards them. 'Is this
true?' she asked, her eyes wide with anxiety. 'Do you
really want her to stay with. . .us?' Breathlessly, she
awaited his reply.

He continued to stare at the gathering dusk, a
thoughtful frown marring his handsome features, his
sensuous mouth twisting slightly as he said, 'It might
be the wisest course.'

Brenda's dark eyes glowed with triumph. 'There now, I *told* you so,' she jeered at Linzi waspishly.

Linzi's heart sank, but her voice remained steady as she said, 'Very well, I'll remove the remainder of my art materials from the third bedroom.' Then her spirits sank even lower as she watched Brenda go to Guy and clasp his arm while laying her dark head against his shoulder.

The sight caused her to rush from the room with tears of frustration blurring her eyes, and as she went to the linen cupboard to find sheets and towels for this unwelcome guest she knew that she had to take a firm grip on herself. If Guy wanted Brenda to stay there was little she herself could do about it. If his contentment lay with this woman there was *nothing* she could do about it, nothing except wish him joy, because even if it broke her heart she wanted him to be happy.

But despite this instinctive altruism where Guy was concerned Linzi found herself in a state of mind that made work at the easel impossible. When she returned to take up her brush she found that her hand had become unsteady, and as she stared at the tree on the canvas her eyes misted to the extent of sending the foliage into a hazy mass of grey-green.

Through the turmoil of her thoughts she heard Brenda's suitcases being carried in from the car. The sound was followed by a murmur of voices in the next room—a murmur which for some reason became dominated by Brenda's rising tones of dissatisfaction.

Listening, although unable to catch the words, Linzi decided that the dark-haired woman's displeasure was caused either by the small size of the room, or by the ever present odour of turps and linseed oil. However, enlightenment came a few minutes later when Guy entered the room.

For several moments his hazel eyes scanned her face as though trying to fathom her thoughts, and then he said, 'Thank you for allowing her to stay.'

'What option did I have?' Linzi snapped from

between tight lips. 'Obviously it was your desire for her to do so.'

He frowned thoughtfully, then admitted, 'Considering she's in an upset state of mind, I felt it was rather late in the day to force her to drive back to Thames. Still. . . I can understand how you feel.'

'Like hell you do.' Linzi snorted wrathfully. 'You haven't the foggiest clue about how that woman's lies have affected me, nor do you understand how I feel about having her in this house.' The last words came bitterly.

'I'll try to make amends,' he promised quietly.

'Really?' She gave a scornful laugh. 'How do you intend to achieve that miracle? I mean, she's *here*, isn't she?'

'Yes, she's here, and I've told her she can stay for a few days while she straightens her mind into some sort of order.'

She looked at him pityingly. 'Can't you see that her mind is already in order? She has a goal and she's heading in a direct line towards it.'

He ignored the comment. 'I've told her that while she's here she must pull her weight, and that *that* means attending to the meals. She was not madly keen about the idea, and was inclined to become somewhat agitated.'

'I heard the raised voice,' Linzi recalled.

Guy went on grimly, 'However, I pointed out that after her constant lying about you she couldn't expect you to rush about preparing her meals—that in fact it was up to her to prepare *your* meals.'

A short laugh escaped Linzi. 'I've no wish to risk being poisoned—but thank you for the admission.'

He frowned. 'Admission? What do you mean?'

'That you now realise that she *has* told lies about me. Honestly, I thought it would never happen.' The clouds that had been pressing her down for so long seemed to lift and drift away, leaving her feeling much happier.

He spoke gruffly. 'Actually, I've been aware of it for

some time.' He paused, then asked significantly, 'How could I believe you had gone away with Shaw when I knew you were here with me?'

'Is that what she told you during those phone calls, as well as when she arrived? Yes, I heard her admit it.'

He nodded, his expression enigmatic.

Her eyes became shadowed. 'Yet after each call you seemed to be in a state of subdued rage with me,' she reminded him, her tone full of reproach.

'Not with you. Honestly, I was infuriated with the situation that had developed around me—'

His words were interrupted by Brenda's appearance in the doorway. She had changed into a full-skirted, strapless red sundress that made her look like a flamboyant gypsy, and her dark eyes flashed from Guy to Linzi as though trying to ascertain the subject of their conversation. Then, when they merely stared at her in silence, she spoke to Guy with cloying sweetness. 'Please come to the kitchen and show me where to find things.'

Linzi felt an unexpected sympathy towards her. 'Perhaps it would be better if I showed you where things are kept,' she offered.

'No, thank you.' The rebuff came sharply as Brenda flicked a derisive glance towards the easel. 'I've no wish to interrupt work on whatever *that's* supposed to be.' Her tone was scathing as she added, 'The sooner it's finished, the sooner you'll be able. . .' Her words trailed away as she sent a significant glance towards Guy.

'To leave for home?' Linzi completed the sentence for her. 'I'm sorry to disappoint you, Brenda, but, as it happens, my work in this place doesn't finish with the painting of this tree.'

Brenda sent another swift glance towards Guy. 'What's she going on about?'

He regarded her calmly. 'Just that she's also working with me.'

The dark eyes widened. 'I don't understand. How can she be working with you? You're writing a *book*.'

Guy spoke patiently, explaining about the illustrations, and as Linzi heard him praise her work she
felt a glow of satisfaction.

Brenda listened with incredulity, her face becoming
a study in discontent, until at last she exclaimed, 'This
I can hardly believe! You're always so—so very reticent
about your books until they are published, yet you'll
allow *her* to look at the manuscript.' She paused, then
demanded almost suspiciously, 'Where are these
sketches? I want to see them.'

Linzi hesitated, feeling that the sketches, like the
manuscript, were not yet for display; therefore she said
to Brenda, 'You'll see them when the book is published.' Then she turned to Guy. 'Am I right?'

'Quite right,' he agreed gravely. 'Nor is it necessary
to have them exposed to disparaging remarks from
people who can't draw a straight line.'

His remark caused Brenda to draw a sharp breath.
'Is it possible you're referring to me?' she demanded
icily.

'More than possible,' Guy retorted harshly. 'Your
comment concerning Linzi's tree held blatant rudeness
that will not be tolerated round these parts, so I'm
warning you to guard that waspish tongue.'

Brenda blinked at him in amazement as she said
plaintively, 'You never used to speak to me like that.'

His mouth tightened. 'No? Well, I'm doing so now.
I'm reminding you that Linzi is the hostess in this
cottage, and if she finds herself unable to abide your
presence you'll leave. It's as simple as that, so you'd
better be polite.'

'I think I know how to behave, thank you very much,
Guy,' Brenda snapped haughtily. And then wisdom
caused her to switch to a more pleasant manner. Taking
his hand, she drew him towards the door as she said
winningly, 'Now may we go to the kitchen? I have to
be shown where things are, remember?'

Linzi felt slightly bewildered as she watched them
leave the room. She appreciated that Guy had champi-

oned her by warning Brenda against further rudeness towards her, but she couldn't help wondering if that had really been on her behalf or if he'd wished to guard against Brenda being expelled from the cottage.

If it had been for the latter reason, she decided, it meant that he genuinely wanted her to be here with him, and the thought sent a twist of pain into Linzi's heart. But overriding every other thought was the knowledge that Brenda was *unmarried*. She had been merely *living* with Garth Shaw, and therefore she was legally free to marry Guy. . .if he asked her to do so.

And there lay the vital question. Did he really love her, or was his feeling for her simply that of long-standing friendship? Only time would tell, Linzi decided with a deep sigh as further depression wrapped itself about her.

She lifted her brush again, dipped it into the darkest green on the palette and made further efforts to strengthen the shadowed areas of the tree's foliage. As she did so the sound of Brenda's shrill laughter echoed from the kitchen. It was enough to tell Linzi that Guy was at least being amicable to his friend of so many years and that he appeared to be coping with the fact that she'd fed him a series of lies. Hadn't he said that he would not tolerate lies?

But of course those lies had concerned herself, Linzi recalled, so perhaps that made them unimportant. Possibly it cast them into the category of white lies, and no doubt he was finding it easy to forgive white lies—especially if there was sufficient reason for them.

A short time later she was assailed by the tantalising aroma of onions being gently fried, and as the domestic scene in the kitchen floated into Linzi's imagination she was seized by a spasm of bitter jealousy. It ate into her soul to the extent of ruining her appetite, so that when Guy appeared in the doorway to tell her the meal was ready she spoke icily, sending him a bleak look.

'I'm not hungry, thank you.'

His eyes narrowed as he stared at her, then he came

further into the room and closed the door behind him. 'What nonsense is this? Of course you're hungry. You haven't eaten for hours.'

She avoided his eyes, which seemed to bore into her. 'I'll survive till the morning, and then I'll find my own breakfast.'

'You'll come and sit at the table right *now*,' he gritted with unconcealed determination.

She shook her head, then spoke frankly. 'If I sit at the table with that woman's black eyes flashing triumph at me I—I might be forced to throw up.'

'Rubbish,' he said sharply, then moved closer to take the paintbrush and palette from her hands. Gripping her elbows, he drew her up from the stool, adding in a low voice, 'Trust me; I promise you everything will be resolved.'

'With wedding bells ringing over your heads?' The uncontrolled words slipped out wrathfully.

He sent her a mirthless grin. 'You'll come to the marriage feast?'

'Not even if you crawled over broken bottles to ask me,' she hissed, her anger almost choking her.

'We'll argue about that when the event occurs.' He grinned with a sparkle of amusement in his eyes. 'In the meantime there's a meal in the kitchen waiting to be eaten.'

She gave in, knowing that further argument would make her appear ungracious. Also, her refusal to come to the table would give Brenda the satisfaction of knowing that her presence was galling to one whom she looked upon as her enemy. Besides, Linzi *was* hungry; therefore she said, 'OK, I'll just wash my hands.'

'Good girl,' he muttered. 'I knew you'd be sensible.'

When she reached the kitchen she found that the table had been nicely set, even to the extent of having a vase of bright yellow and orange nasturtiums at its centre. Aunt Bea's best dinner-set had been taken from the dining-room sideboard, and the plates were filled with a tasty meal of grilled steak, tomatoes, peas and mashed potatoes. Fried onions added flavour to the gravy.

'I shall enjoy this,' Guy said as he sat down.

Brenda spoke quickly. 'That sounds as if your previous meals have been unsatisfactory. Does it mean that Linzi can't cook?'

Linzi ignored the veiled attack, but Guy did not let it pass. 'You are mistaken,' he said tightly. 'We have eaten more than adequately, and for your information Linzi is a very good cook.'

Linzi looked at him gratefully, but still she said nothing. She was finding difficulty in eating, and although the steak was deliciously tender she seemed unable to swallow the food.

Brenda spoke to Guy in a seductive tone. 'Haven't we any wine? This meal is really a celebration. We should open a bottle of red.' Her dark eyes glowed as she looked at him.

Surprise caused his brows to rise. 'Celebration? What—exactly—are we celebrating?'

'The first meal I've cooked for you, of course, although I didn't expect it to be shared by a third party.' Brenda flicked a reproachful glance towards Linzi.

'I'm afraid we're out of wine,' Guy retorted briefly.

Brenda made an effort to pout prettily. 'That's a pity. Still, I'm hoping it'll be the first of many meals to come, and at least you can see that I can take care of a man's culinary needs.' She paused, then sent him an arch glance, adding coyly, 'I can also take care of his every other comfort. . .and *need*.'

Linzi could scarcely believe her ears. She felt slightly shocked because Brenda's words had sounded like an open invitation to the bedroom, and she waited anxiously for Guy's reaction.

His expression remained unfathomable as he spoke to Brenda silkily. 'In that case why has Shaw left you?'

Brenda drew a long, deep breath. 'Because he's

searching for *her*.' She spat the words venomously while glaring at Linzi.

'Then he's wasting his time,' Linzi retorted sharply. 'He's been told often enough that I'll have nothing to do with him, so don't you *dare* accuse me of enticing him away.' The outburst left her feeling so shaken that she was unable to eat another mouthful; therefore she laid down her knife and fork and pushed her chair back.

But before she could leave the table Guy placed a detaining hand on her arm. 'You haven't finished your meal,' he said pointedly.

Her expression became pathetic. 'I can't eat any more.'

He spoke sternly. 'Your body needs food even if your mind tells you it doesn't. Besides, the problem will disappear tomorrow.'

'Disappear?' Linzi asked with faint surprise. 'What do you mean?'

'Yes, exactly what *do* you mean?' Brenda demanded apprehensively.

Guy turned to her. 'Just that you'll be with your parents. Or have you forgotten they live in Coromandel?'

Brenda was visibly perturbed. 'No—please, Guy—I don't want to go to them. You said I could stay here, remember?'

His voice hardened. 'There was a condition of civility attached to that, which you also appear to have forgotten. Really, Brenda, you surprise me. I thought I knew you...but now I realise I've never known you at all.' His brows drew together as he stared at her.

Brenda became even more agitated as she began to plead, 'Please, Guy, I don't want my parents to know that Garth and I have broken up. They never did approve of him. But I've been so unhappy, and it's because of his chasing after Linzi that I've come to you. I know you'll give me stability and security. You're so steadfast. And I'll be polite...that's a promise.'

'It had better be kept,' he snarled.

She went on. 'You do understand how insecure I've felt? And now I doubt that he'll come back to me. Please, Guy, don't send me away.'

He looked at her morosely but said nothing.

Next day Linzi noticed that Brenda took care to offer her more friendship, although she sensed that it was only on a surface that would not bear scratching. She also noticed that Brenda spent time in the dining room. Did this mean that Guy did not mind the disruption and that her company was more important than his work? Did it also mean that his old affection for Brenda was beginning to reassert itself? The fear swirled in her mind as she put the finishing touches to the highlights of the pohutukawa tree.

Engrossed, she did not become aware of Guy's presence until his deep voice spoke to her from the doorway, where he stood viewing her work.

'Surely that's finished?' he said. 'It needs only your signature.'

Ignoring the wild fluttering that rose within her, she glanced over her shoulder. As usual the sight of his handsome face and virile body caused her heart to skip a beat, but she managed to speak calmly. 'Yes, it's finished. I shall now clean my palette and brushes, and then I'll work on the gold-mining sketches.'

He came further into the room for a closer scrutiny of the gnarled trunk, the twisted branches and crimson flowers, then informed her casually, 'Brenda and I are going over the hill to the town. We need to buy food. She says that if she has to cook it she'd prefer to choose it.'

'That sounds reasonable.' Linzi kept her tone light, but only with an effort 'Brenda and I'. The phrase appeared to slip from his lips so naturally. Nor was there any suggestion that she should accompany them, she noticed, then reminded herself that she had no wish to be relegated to the back seat of the car while Brenda sat beside Guy. Instinct warned that this was sure to happen, because in Guy's mind she had been taking a back seat to Brenda from the first moment of their acquaintance.

A short time later she stood at the window to watch the car leave the driveway and disappear along the road. Depression descended as it turned the corner, and despite her efforts to shake it off she was gripped by a sense of loss that was so intense that it brought tears to her eyes.

'You're being a prize idiot,' she chided herself furiously in a voice that echoed across the room. 'You can't lose what you've never had. Jealousy will get you nowhere.'

But the advice gave her no comfort, and at last she set her mind to the cleaning task, scraping the remaining paint from her palette and carrying it with her brushes to the laundry, where she washed them with turpentine.

But the tears continued to stream down her cheeks until she dashed them away with a gesture of impatience. Nevertheless, they did a certain amount of good because the short bout of weeping was sufficient to relieve her feelings, even if it did put her into a state of resigned hopelessness. But that was something she did her best to ignore, and within a short time she was busily sketching from the photos that had been taken in the museum.

The cartoons also came in for her attention, and eventually the amusement of doing them caused all trace of tears to disappear. At the same time her ears were kept open for the sound of the returning car, and when she heard it turn into the drive the cartoons were hastily slipped into the back of her sketching-pad.

Listening from the settee in the lounge where she had now settled herself, she heard bundles being dumped on the kitchen table. Moments later Guy came to see what she was doing, and, as was to be expected, he was followed by Brenda.

He nodded his approval of the sketches while comparing them with the photos; then, showing them to Brenda, he said, 'You can see how they'll enhance the ends of the chapters.'

Brenda gave a girlish laugh. 'I'm afraid I can't see that at all. Personally, I think you'd be wiser to just use the photos and leave these silly little sketches out altogether.' For the moment her new-found friendliness towards Linzi seemed to be slipping.

Linzi looked at her but said nothing, waiting for Guy's response. Would he be swayed by Brenda's opinion? she wondered anxiously. Or would he recognise it as antagonism aimed at her? If he agreed with Brenda she would pack her belongings and leave this evening because, with her two paintings finished, she would have no reason to remain in this house. She held her breath, trying to read the expression on his face.

Guy held the pad lightly, examining the top page, which had several small items sketched on it. There was a tense silence while he frowned thoughtfully, then he said, 'I like the idea of appropriate sketches at chapter endings, especially if there's a blank space left on the page. In any case I've already made an arrangement with Linzi and I shall not go back on my word, especially as she has already put work into the project.'

Brenda gave another girlish laugh. 'Work? You call this *work*?' she demanded impatiently, then almost snatched the pad for a closer examination of the sketches.

As she did so the cartoons in the back slipped out to fall on the floor, fanning out to lie face upwards and reveal the character of the drawings.

Linzi shot from the settee to scoop them up, but before she could reach them Guy had pounced upon them. 'What are these?' he demanded, staring at them with undisguised surprise.

'They're just private drawings of my own,' she replied hastily.

'But they're about gold-mining,' he pointed out suspiciously. 'What do you intend to do with them—?'

'*That*, surely, is obvious,' Brenda cut in with decision. 'She intends to compile a book of cartoons. Naturally, the ideas have all come from your book, and that makes them *stolen* ideas, which sounds very much like *plagiarism* to me.'

Linzi went scarlet with fury. 'How dare you make such an accusation?' she lashed at Brenda. Then she swung round to face Guy. 'Do you also believe this nonsense?' she demanded wrathfully, her eyes flashing blue-green sparks. 'If you do I shall leave at once and take all my sketches with me.'

Brenda laughed. 'Aha! There speaks a guilty conscience.'

'Shut up, Brenda,' Guy rasped. Then to Linzi he said, 'How can I know what to think? Why don't you simmer down and tell me what put the idea of cartoons into your head?'

'Actually it was the desire to sketch something more interesting than sluice-boxes and panning dishes. Would it be too much for you to understand that the humorous patches in your own manuscript set me off?'

'There now!' Brenda exclaimed. 'I *told* you so.'

Linzi ignored her. 'My imagination saw a little man doing all the things he'd dreamed of doing. . .like finding a nugget that was too large to hide or drag to the bank. And then one idea led to another.'

Guy was grinning broadly as he examined the sketches. 'They're really very good. So what *do* you intend doing with them?' The question came casually.

'Only one thing: when I'd completed about a dozen I intended offering them to you to use or discard as you wished.' Linzi hesitated, then admitted, 'I haven't shown them to you before because I feared you might think they'd lower the tone of your book.'

Brenda spoke coldly. 'For once you are right. Cartoons have no place in any of Guy's books—have they, darling?' She turned to him with wide-eyed appeal.

'Darling'? The endearment jarred on Linzi, causing her to glance from one to the other. Did this mean that their relationship had advanced during the short shopping period? But she was unable to tell because Brenda's lips were curved in an enigmatic smile while Guy's face had become inscrutable.

Brenda went on hastily, almost as though pressing home an advantage, 'Guy has been so *sweet* to me this afternoon... He knows that I'm so proud of his published works...and that I couldn't *bear* the standard to be lowered by *cartoons*.' She clasped his arm and gazed up into his face. 'You will be sensible about this, Guy, *dear*?'

He sent her an amused glance while gently disengaging his arm. 'I'll give it careful consideration,' he promised. 'However, I think your own suggestion is quite a good one.'

'My suggestion?' Brenda regarded him blankly, obviously trying to recall any suggestion she had made, then as the answer evaded her she said, 'I'm glad if I've been helpful, but I can't remember making a suggestion.'

'It was the one about Linzi compiling a book of cartoons,' Guy reminded her. 'Personally, I don't believe she had any intention of doing so. I feel sure the sketches were meant for me, as she claims. She is not a devious person.'

Linzi felt a surge of relief. She looked at him gratefully as she said, 'Thank you for having that much faith in me, Guy. Does that mean you'll accept them for inclusion in your book?'

He shook his head. 'No, their place is not in my book. The better plan is for you to complete more of them and compile your own book, as Brenda suggested.'

Linzi gaped at him. 'You really believe I should do that?' she exclaimed incredulously, her spirits suddenly uplifted.

'Of course. These samples show you have the ability,

plus the necessary sense of humour to go with it.' He stared at one of the drawings and began to laugh heartily.

Brenda was irritated by his mirth. She spoke crossly. 'I see nothing amusing in them. In fact I consider them to be utterly childish—but then we don't all see humour in the same way, do we?' she added, as though making an effort to soften her criticism.

Guy agreed with her. 'That's true, and when Linzi has completed sufficient sketches they'll be put to the test. They'll be sent to my publisher to see if he can get a laugh out of them. I've heard him say that humour sells well.'

Brenda turned to Linzi, her manner having changed from her former veiled derision. 'Linzi, dear, I do hope you have success with them,' she said in a tone that held sweetness.

'Thank you,' Linzi murmured. She was not fooled. She knew that Brenda's good wishes had little sincerity in them, and that they had been voiced merely for Guy's benefit.

She noticed that he was still smiling over the cartoons. It was all she needed to give her encouragement and to send excitement surging through her. Her chin lifted as a flush touched her cheeks, and her eyes shone as she spoke to him. 'Perhaps we could work together on more of them?' The question came timidly.

'Yes, we'll do that,' he enthused. 'It'll be fun thinking up pithy captions. No doubt we should thank Brenda for the idea of putting your cartoons into a book.'

Brenda spoke quickly. 'I'm glad to hear you admit it was my idea because that means I must be included in the project. Whenever you are working on it together I shall expect to be with you.' She turned to Linzi, adding with more sweetness, 'I hope you realise that Guy and I are together now, so you'll just have to get used to seeing me around.' She looked at him with wide-eyed appeal. 'Isn't that so, dear?'

Guy said nothing, his face holding an inscrutable

expression until suddenly it broke into a grin. He then strode from the room.

Linzi felt irritated by his action. Why couldn't he say something one way or the other?

CHAPTER TEN

WHEN Linzi woke next morning the thought of Brenda's continued presence in Kauri Cottage was enough to make her cower beneath the blankets. Nor had there been any comfort in Guy's reaction to the dark-haired woman's assertion that they were together. Why had he grinned? What was funny about the situation? Or had his grin expressed delight at the prospect of having Brenda around at last?

Sighing, she left her bed and went to the window, where she looked out at a sky that was overcast. The distant hills were a sombre dark blue that heralded rain, and the air was oppressive with a humidity that caused her to suspect that the peninsula was about to receive one of its summer thunderstorms complete with lightning.

Later, when she went to the kitchen, she found Brenda and Guy still at breakfast, the plates before them showing signs of bacon and eggs, sausages and tomatoes. Guy stood up and pulled out a chair for her, while Brenda offered a polite good morning.

The dark-haired woman then continued her conversation with Guy. 'What shall we be doing today?' she queried in an eager voice that was full of expectation.

Guy gave a small grimace. 'I can assure you that my day is already well planned. It will be spent in the dining room at the word processor.'

'But not the entire day,' Brenda protested in a voice that sounded pained. 'Can't you spare time to be with me? Don't you realise I've come here to be with you?' she exclaimed in a reproachful tone. 'I was hoping we could drive along the coast road to the top end of the peninsula. I'll make sandwiches to take with us. I mean just the *two* of us, of course.'

Listening, Linzi paused while pouring milk on a mixture of cornflakes, dried fruits and nuts, holding her breath, waiting for Guy's reply. Would he comply with Brenda's request? Driving to the northern tip of the peninsula would take hours from his work, and she felt that if he agreed to go the answer to whether or not he had any feelings for Brenda would become clear.

He frowned, uttering a reply that had a negative ring in its very abruptness. 'Sorry, Brenda, I have no intention of taking that sort of time away from my work. I'm surprised that you would expect me to.'

Brenda's childish pout played about her lips. 'No doubt you've had plenty of interruptions recently,' she remarked, flicking a baleful glance towards Linzi.

The hint hit home, causing Linzi to feel guilty because she knew that she had been the prime cause of the interruptions to Guy's work. And then his next words made her wonder if he'd read her thoughts.

Speaking to Brenda, he said, 'As it happens, there is a short trip to be made today. You may come with me when I return the crutches I borrowed when Linzi sprained her ankle.'

'There's no need for you to do that,' Linzi hastened to inform him. 'I used the crutches, so I'll return them to the convalescent home. It's only right that I should do so.'

Guy spoke with determination. 'I prefer to see to it myself. As I borrowed them, it's my responsibility to return them.'

Brenda laid a hand on his arm as she gazed into his face. 'May we go *alone*?' she pleaded.

'I suppose so,' he conceded gruffly. Then, turning to Linzi, he said nonchalantly, 'We'll be away for only a short time.'

She was in the grip of extreme irritation, but she kept her temper as she said with forced sweetness, 'Don't mind me. Just take as long as you please. In fact, take all day and all night if it makes you happy to do so.'

He sent her a long, searching look. 'Do you really mean that?'

Her chin rose. 'Why shouldn't I mean it?' Then she avoided his penetrating gaze by leaving the table and taking her now empty bowl to the sink. After that she poured herself a cup of tea, then said, 'If you'll excuse me I'll take this to my room.'

'Don't you want toast and marmalade to go with it?' Guy asked.

'No, thank you.' The only thing she wanted was to get away from the gloating black eyes that followed her about the room, to say nothing of the smile of triumph that hovered about Brenda's thin lips. Nor did the memory of them vanish when she reached her bedroom. Instead they continued to niggle at her until she was gripped by a burning anger.

It was an anger that also spread towards Guy, and despite her love for him she felt that he was being overbearing and ridiculous. There was no reason why she should not return the crutches, and the more she thought about it, the more rebellious she became, until, fired by resentment, she came to a decision. She *would* return them herself.

It took only seconds to find her car keys and to take the crutches from where they leaned against the wall in a corner of the room. Then she carried them to the kitchen, where Brenda and Guy were about to leave the table after loitering there for longer than usual.

Guy frowned when he saw the crutches, and sent Linzi a questioning glance as he said, 'Don't tell me where you're going—let me guess.'

'That's easy!' Brenda exclaimed. 'She's returning the crutches, of course. She's deliberately defying you.'

'I don't expect Linzi to obey me,' he retorted sharply. 'However, I'd be interested to learn why she's so determined to go against my wishes. I thought I'd made them clear enough.'

Brenda gave a sardonic laugh. 'Can't you see it's to

remove your reason for taking me out? Not that it will, Guy, dear. I know you'll take me just the same.'

But it seemed as if Guy hardly heard her because he continued to stare at Linzi as though expecting an answer. 'Well?' he demanded at last with a wry twist of his lips.

Linzi returned his gaze dumbly while raking about in her mind for a plausible reply. She had no intention of admitting that her action had been prompted by an inner fusion of resentment and jealousy, and she breathed a sigh of relief as an inspiration gave her an answer.

'It's my car,' she said. 'The motor hasn't been turned over since I've been here. If I don't give it a run I might be faced with a flat battery.' Then she left them and carried the crutches out to where the car was parked.

She placed them in the back, then took her seat behind the wheel. But when she turned on the ignition nothing happened. The battery was indeed flat. Frustrated, she tried again and again until, glancing about her, she saw that the switch of the inside light had been left on.

She then recalled that it had been dusk when she'd arrived, and that she had turned it on while emptying the car. No doubt the shock of finding Guy already in the house had made her forget to switch it off; therefore she had only herself to blame for this irritating situation of having to face Guy and admit that she was unable to return the crutches.

When she did so his face remained expressionless, while Brenda almost doubled up with mirth, until Guy snarled at her, 'Shut up, Brenda. Just get yourself into the car and we'll go at once. I'm sure Linzi won't mind clearing the breakfast dishes.'

Linzi nodded wordlessly, then began stacking the plates. A few minutes later she watched the car leave the backyard, and as it passed the kitchen window she caught a glimpse of Brenda's face turning to gaze at

Guy. She also saw the smile that hovered about his lips, and it was sufficient to fill her with despondency.

This was not because he had requested her to attend to the dishes, which, with a dishwasher in the house, was a quick and simple task. It was because he had no wish for her to accompany them, and that seemed to prove beyond all doubt that he desired to be alone with Brenda. The knowledge caused physical as well as mental pain.

Linzi could have tolerated this situation more easily if Brenda had been a nicer woman—one whom she considered capable of making Guy happy. But she doubted that Guy was seeing her clearly. She feared that he was being blinded by the nostalgia of their earlier years when his parents had been alive.

It would also have been easier to bear if her own love for him hadn't been growing more intense with every passing day. But that was an emotion that she was unable to turn on and off like a tap, and she was beginning to wonder how it would affect the rest of her life. Would she eventually get over it, or was she destined to endure the coming years loving someone who didn't love her?

The question made her feel even more miserable, and she realised that the sooner she got away from the sight of Brenda and Guy together, the better it would be for her own peace of mind. But first she must finish his sketches, and then seek his aid in getting her car running.

She was at work in the lounge when she heard the slam of a car door. A rapid glance at her watch showed it to be too soon for their return...unless Guy had changed his mind about her being with them and had come back to fetch her. The thought made her heart leap. She dropped her pencil and sprang up to look out of the window, but was unable to see the car parked on the driveway. Moments later a man stepped onto the veranda, and Linzi was horrified to see that it was Garth Shaw.

He paused, his pale blue eyes full of surprise as he caught sight of her at the window, then he sauntered through the open front door to face her in the lounge. 'Well, well, well,' he drawled. 'Fancy finding you here. What is this—a harem?'

'I don't know what you're talking about,' Linzi snapped indignantly. 'Nor have you any right to walk into this house. I did not invite you—'

'You can climb down from your high perch and tell me where they are,' he interrupted impatiently. 'I'm talking about Brenda and the man she's never got out of her system,' he snarled.

'Brenda's not here—' she began.

'Don't give me that lie,' he rasped, coming a step closer and glaring at her. 'Her car is at the end of the drive.'

She looked at him wonderingly. 'How did you know—?'

'That's not your concern. The point is that I know she is here, and I want to know the situation between her and Nelson.' His eyes narrowed. 'Perhaps you can tell me.'

'Whatever it is, it is their concern,' she retorted loftily. 'I've no wish to discuss it. However, she did say she'd left you, and that it was all over between you.'

'Is that so? Then tell me, has she been sleeping with him?' he demanded in a low voice.

The mere question gave Linzi a pain that went straight to her heart. 'I don't know,' she admitted. 'I'm not in the habit of creeping about at night to discover where people are sleeping.' Then she added scathingly, 'In any case, you're a fine specimen to be criticising her activities. I have very clear recollections of your own.'

He grinned as though her words had pleased him. 'Something of a Casanova, am I?' he smirked.

Linzi spoke coldly. 'You might look upon yourself as a great lover, but you don't impress me. What's more, you'll have to talk hard and fast to convince Brenda. Her sights have become set in another direction.'

'Upon Nelson, I suppose.' Garth scowled. 'She was always throwing his success and his wealth at me. I dare say I'll learn to put up with it. It gave me a shock when I found she'd taken off during my absence,' he admitted gloomily.

'So where were you?' Linzi tried to sound casual. There was no need to expound on Brenda's lies about his having gone away with herself, she decided.

Garth gave a slight shrug. 'I merely went on one of my usual short trips to Auckland. I needed to choose framing materials.'

Linzi believed him. She herself was in the habit of taking similar trips to the wholesalers of mouldings and mountboards. Nevertheless she said, 'So why didn't you tell her where you were going?'

'Because we'd had a quarrel,' he admitted in an aggrieved tone. 'But we usually get over them, so there was no need for her to dash off and to take most of her clothes.' He shook his head dolefully. 'I'm afraid she really has left me. She's flown to his lordship.'

'You have only yourself to blame,' Linzi pointed out gently. 'Why you persisted in pursuing me as you did I'll never know.' Strangely, she was even beginning to feel sorry for him.

He took a few strides closer, his hands reaching out to grip her arms. 'The answer to that is simple,' he said, staring down into her face. 'You're lovely to look at, and I'll not deny you do something to me, but my main reason lay in making Brenda jealous. All she could do was extol the virtues of Nelson. I felt I had to retaliate in some way and you were close at hand. Do you understand?'

'No, I do not,' she responded angrily, wrenching her arms from his grasp. Despite the fact that he clearly wanted Brenda back, she could see that he was still a danger to herself. And if Guy and Brenda returned to find them together heaven alone knew what they would imagine—possibly that he had come to find *her* rather than Brenda. Whatever they thought, it would be the worst.

The thought of such a situation horrified her. Brenda's accusations would be shouted aloud, and Guy would believe them. Panic gripped her and she knew she must do something. . .but what? She also knew that getting rid of Garth before he'd spoken to Brenda would be impossible; therefore she must distance herself from him.

Thinking rapidly she recalled the cave in the hills beyond the back of the cottage. If she could reach it unseen it would serve as a place of refuge until Guy returned; therefore she pointed to an easy chair and said, 'Sit there. I'll make you some coffee.'

He smirked. 'I'll expect more than coffee from Brenda when I get her home. . .that's *if* I can get her home.'

She ignored his doubts, leaving the room and making her way to the kitchen, but to her dismay he did not sit down. He followed her. The instant coffee took only a few minutes to make, then she carried a small tray with two steaming mugs back to the lounge. Placing it on a table, she asked, 'Sugar? I'm afraid I've forgotten it.'

'No, thank you.'

'Oh, well, I do. I'll just fetch it.'

She left the room without any sign of haste, but when she reached the kitchen she slipped through the door quietly, then ran towards the place where she knew the track used to be, and where she and Guy had pushed their way through the long grass towards the high face with its areas of rock and scrubby growth. As she did so there was a vivid flash of lightning, followed almost immediately by a reverberating crash of thunder that seemed to be directly overhead. It almost sent her heart into her mouth, and as she glanced up she realised that the ominous dark clouds of the morning had developed into the promised thunderstorm that now boomed like a battlefield.

Linzi hated thunder and lightning, and as more

deafening claps followed brilliant flashes and vibrated against the hills she tried to hasten her steps towards the cave. But before she reached it the rain began to fall, coming down in great drenching torrents that soaked her summer dress within minutes.

She reached the cave at last, and, desperate for shelter, she rushed beneath the protection of its roof, completely forgetting the state of its floor. Granted, the water they had seen previously had drained away, but, as Guy had predicted, the mud was too deep to walk across. And Linzi was stuck in it.

Disconcerted, she looked down at her legs to discover the silt almost reaching her calves. And although she tried to lift one foot it seemed to be gripped by a strong suction that held it firmly. She tried to move the other foot, with a similar result, and cursed herself roundly for rushing so stupidly into the cave without thought.

A feeling of helplessness overwhelmed her, causing her to look about her in desperation until she noticed that one side of the wall had a low shelf cut into it. It ran from near the entrance towards the back of the cave, where it fell away to nothing, and had possibly been formed to enable probing for gold at a higher level.

But now it would serve as a seat. . .if only she could reach it. In fact she knew she *had* to reach it, otherwise she might sink further down and be here until her bones were found at some distant date in the future. The thought sent panic into her mind, causing her to make supreme efforts to drag one foot after the other in mud-sinking steps that took her towards the side of the cave. Her shoes were lost in the slow struggle to get there, but at last she scrambled onto the shelf, which was at least a yard wide.

Relief flooded her as she leaned her back against the earth wall, and although she knew that the problem of getting out of this muddy place lay before her she pushed it aside and closed her eyes, listening to the steady fall of the rain. Was it becoming less heavy? Perhaps the storm was passing. And then the next hour dragged slowly.

Fortunately the air was warm, and within a short time her clothes began to feel less damp. And despite the earthy odour arising from the mud a drowsiness crept over her. But she knew she must not allow herself to doze, otherwise she might fall off the shelf.

Nevertheless she continued to feel dreamy, and her thoughts drifted back to the day when she had shown this place to Guy. He had told her about fool's gold, she recalled. He had kissed her and held her against him, and even now the memory of his desire sent a warm sensation sweeping through her body, clawing at her stomach.

But the emotions he felt for her did not add up to real love. They were little more than fool's gold when compared with the commitment she needed from him. . .and which she knew she could forget about.

'Linzi. . .' The voice came faintly from the distance.

Her eyes flew open as she realised that Garth was out looking for her. Crouching on her seat, she remained silent.

'Linzi, where are you. . .?'

This time the voice was close enough to be identified. Relief and then excitement filled her as she raised her own voice and shouted, 'Guy, I'm in the cave.'

Moments later he arrived at the entrance, where he stood staring at her with amazement. 'What the hell are you doing in there?' he demanded, his eyes moving to rest on her muddy legs.

'I—I wanted to get away from Garth,' she explained weakly. 'And then the rain came and I ran for shelter.'

'Well, it has stopped now. The sun is shining, in case you haven't noticed.' He peered at her intently. 'Did Shaw make a pest of himself?'

'No, but I feared that his mind could be edging towards it.' She paused, then went on frankly, 'I also

knew that if you came home and found us together
you'd be sure to imagine the worst.'

'Why would I do that?'

'Because you've done nothing else,' she flashed at
him. 'In fact you would probably think I had phoned to
let him know I was here.' Her last words were filled
with a bitterness that revealed the hurt she felt.

'I'd be unlikely to do that,' he drawled. 'I know
exactly why Shaw is here. He has come to persuade
Brenda to return to him. They're arguing about it now.'

'Do you think she'll go with him?' Linzi's question
came anxiously.

Guy gave a small shrug. 'Her choice lies between
returning to him or going to her parents.'

'Garth. . .or her *parents*?' She hesitated, looking at
him wide-eyed, then asked timidly, 'You haven't
invited her to stay with you? I mean. . .you don't *want*
her to be with you?'

'Certainly not. If you come out here I'll explain why.
Or do you intend to remain there for the rest of the
day?'

'Heaven forbid—but I have to get through that mud
to reach the entrance. It should give you a good laugh.
I've already lost my shoes, but fortunately they were
old ones.'

Guy calculated the distance between the shelf and
the opening, then said, 'I could fetch the long ladder
from the garage. If it reaches you could crawl along it.'

But Linzi was gripped by a surge of impatience to
learn his reason for not wanting Brenda to be with him;
therefore she said, 'No, please don't bother about the
ladder. I've been through the mud once, so I can do it
again.' It was difficult to keep her eagerness hidden as
she slid from the shelf and made slow, dragging steps
towards the cave entrance.

Guy stretched his arms to grip her hands as she
reached it, then gently pulled her towards him. His
arms slid around her to draw her closer to him, and as
he looked down into her face his deep voice came

huskily. 'Can't you guess why I've no wish for Brenda to be with me? It should be easy for you to do so.'

She gazed up at him wonderingly, then shook her head in a bewildered manner. 'I—I'm afraid I'm not very good at guessing.'

'Can't you see that there's somebody else I'd prefer to have beside me for the rest of my life?'

Somebody else? Who could he mean? Surely not *herself*? An intense excitement began to dance through her veins but she kept it under control by refusing to allow herself to be carried away by wishful thinking. And then the memory of previous events caused her to say, 'I felt sure it was Brenda you wanted—this friend of such long standing whose lies you've persisted in believing. . .'

'Not any more—and I can only ask you to forgive me for doing so.' His voice held a ring of sincerity, and his eyes became piercing as he asked, 'Do you remember the last time we were here?'

'Vividly. You spoke of your caveman act.' Memory of the hurt she had felt at the time now echoed in her voice.

'I'm afraid I approached the subject badly. Actually, I was about to tell you *then* what I'm about to tell you *now*, but on that day you took off in a rage.'

'You mean you were about to tell me about this person you'd like to have beside you?' A strange feeling came over her as she recalled that day when she'd fled back to the cottage with tears streaming down her face. Her mind had been full of presumptions, and she'd given him no chance for further explanation.

And now, although her heart was beginning to beat more rapidly, she knew that she must not make the same mistake of allowing presumption to take over. She must not jump to the conclusion that she was the person he meant. She had to hear him say the words.

And then they came as his voice cut into her thoughts. 'Darling, don't you realise that you are that person? Can't you see that I love you. . .and that I can't live without you?' His voice had become unsteady as he stared down into her face. 'Do you think you could stay beside me for ever?'

Her heart seemed to swell to bursting point, her face becoming radiant as she said tremulously, 'Oh, yes. . . yes. . . I reckon I could manage for ever. . .and ever. . .'

'You could? Does that mean. . .?'

'That I love you? Yes, it does. I love you very much, Guy.' A deep sigh escaped her as the words came tumbling out. 'It's so wonderful to be able to tell you at last.' She lifted her face for his kiss, which was long and deep with a mounting passion.

At last he murmured against her lips, 'How soon can we be married, my dear one? You will marry me, I hope?'

His words sent her up into the clouds. 'Yes. . .yes. . . as soon as my parents return from Australia and arrangements can be made,' she promised, then paused before adding thoughtfully, 'I'd like it to be in the church where Aunt Bea and Richard were married.'

'Naturally. It couldn't be anywhere else,' he assured her.

There was no mention of that having been the place where he had first indicated his disapproval of her and where the antagonism between them had begun. They simply clung to each other in an ecstasy of joy, murmuring endearments between the kisses that wafted Linzi into a state of delirious excitement as the desire to make love with Guy throbbed through her body.

But at last he put her from him with a firm movement, saying with decision, 'We must return to the cottage. Your clothes are still damp and I've no wish for a bride with pneumonia. Besides, I must learn how the argument between Brenda and Shaw is progressing.' Then he took her hand and began to lead her away from the cave opening.

His last words had brought her down to earth, causing her to admit with a shaky laugh, 'These last few minutes had made me forget about them. Will you tell them about us?'

'Of course. Why not?'

She became apprehensive. 'Because the thought of Brenda's reaction frightens me. Apparently you meant so much to each other in the past, and now she's come here to be with you, remember?'

He stopped suddenly, then swung round to face her, his expression grim as he said, 'Then hear this, my darling. We were never lovers. . .nor was I ever in love with her. We were just good friends, but even that relationship has evaporated on account of the lies she has told me.'

Linzi breathed a sigh of relief. The thought of Guy and Brenda having been lovers at some previous time had been one of her secret torments, but now that he had dissolved that cloud she went towards the cottage with more confidence.

When they reached the back of the house she washed the mud from her legs and feet at an outside tap, then went to the bathroom for a quick shower. She kenw that Brenda and Garth were still arguing because she could hear their raised voices, and while dressing in her bedroom she caught scraps of the conversation coming across the passage.

Garth's voice came clearly. 'I'm asking you again to come home with me. Everything will be different, I promise.'

'I don't believe you, so I'm staying with Guy,' Brenda snapped.

'Has he asked you to marry him?' Garth sounded amused.

'No, but he will.' Her tone was full of assurance.

The words then became mumbled until Garth said, 'When I came home and found you'd really gone I nearly went mad.'

'How was I to know you'd gone to Auckland? Why should I believe you now?' Her voice had become plaintive.

'For Pete's sake, woman, the stock I brought home will prove it. And there's something else about Auckland—something I haven't told you. It was to be a surprise for you.'

'You have a woman there as well? *That* would be no surprise.' Her words came scathingly.

'Of course not. Brenda. . .darling. . .come home with me. I promise there'll never be another woman. You're the only one I want.'

A derisive laugh echoed across the passage as she said, 'That's what you say now, but how can I believe it will last?'

'Because I'm *promising* you.' His voice had a sincere ring to it.

There was a silence until she said, 'So what else is there about Auckland. . .and what makes you think I'll be interested?'

'The fact that I might go there. The wholesalers told me about a framing business that's for sale. It belongs to an old chap who has plans to retire and move from the city. The price is within my reach, so I had a look at it while I was there. It was what delayed my return home. Actually, I've almost decided to take it on.'

'Then you can go there alone.' Brenda's voice quavered. 'I've told you I'm staying with Guy. He's reliable and has integrity. Can't you see I need someone I can depend upon?' she added tearfully.

At that moment Guy appeared in Linzi's doorway. He stood still, gazing at her freshened appearance, then came into the bedroom and took her in his arms. 'Did you hear what Brenda said?' he whispered against her ear, holding her closely.

She nodded wordlessly, savouring the feel of his body pressing against her own; then she said, 'I feel sorry for her.'

'Are you ready to help me change her mind?'

'Of course. Haven't I promised to be at your side from now onwards?'

His lips found hers possessively for several long

moments before he released her gently. 'OK, let's get it over with,' he said. Then he took her hand and they crossed the passage to enter the lounge.

They found Brenda standing at the window with her back to them while Garth leaned against the mantelpiece. He looked frustrated and as though his temper was being held in check only with difficulty.

Brenda swung round to face them, then crossed the room to stand before Guy. She took a deep breath then said plaintively, 'Guy, darling, I want you to tell Garth about us—that we...that we...' The words faltered and died on her lips as she suddenly realised that Guy and Linzi were holding hands.

Guy's voice rang with firm determination. 'There's nothing to tell him about you and me, Brenda, apart from what has been cooked up in your own mind. And we all know how fertile your imagination can be. You'd be very wise to fall in with his plans.'

Brenda flushed but could find no reply. Her jaw sagged slightly and her eyes narrowed as she stared suspiciously at Linzi's shining eyes and radiant face. 'You...and her?' she croaked at last.

Guy answered her calmly. 'Yes. For your information Linzi and I are to be married. I love her very dearly. I can't wait to make her my wife.'

'That's a jolly good idea,' Garth applauded heartily. He turned to Brenda. 'Now that you know the situation perhaps you'll have enough sense to come to Auckland with me. Let's make a new start by getting married at once.'

Brenda stared at him with amazement. 'You're actually ready to get married...at last? You'll really give me a feeling of definite security...at last? Garth... dear...why didn't you say so before?'

Garth frowned. 'You know damned well that I've been ready for a long time. It was you who kept putting it off...and we've both known why.' He sent a dark scowl towards Guy.

Brenda spoke hastily. 'Well, that's finished now. I'll

promise to forget *him* if you'll promise to forget *her*.
It's a deal? If so I'm more than ready to make a fresh
start in Auckland.'

Garth grinned, then gave Brenda a brief hug. 'OK,
it's a deal. Now throw your things together and we'll
get the hell out of here.'

A short time later Guy and Linzi stood at the lounge
window to watch Brenda's car sweep out of the driveway. It was followed by Garth's vehicle, and as the
latter disappeared Linzi said, 'I can't understand how
he knew she was here.'

Guy gave a short laugh. 'The answer to that is simple.
He knew because I phoned and told him to come and
take her away.'

'You did?' Linzi was unable to hide her surprise.
'But you took her to return the crutches instead of
me. . .'

'I did that because I needed to talk to her. I wanted
to impress upon her the fact that the thought she had
in mind concerning myself were quite hopeless. It was
an attempt to make her see sense, and to put her into a
more receptive mood to meet Shaw when he arrived.
However, I'm afraid my words made little impression
on her. She kept insisting that I'd remained single
because of her, which is utter rot.'

'I sometimes wondered if that had been the case,'
Linzi admitted.

'Definitely not,' he declared crisply. 'I was waiting
for the right woman to come along, and then one day I
saw her right beside me, busily sketching. It was soon
after you arrived here.'

'Then why were you always so cross with me?' she
demanded quietly.

'You can put it down to raging jealousy. The thought
of you having an affair with Shaw nearly drove me up
the wall.'

'I did try to tell you. . .' she reminded him.

'I know.' His tone held remorse. 'But my mind had
been poisoned by an expert who, thankfully, will be

leaving Thames to live in Auckland, and therefore out of our lives.'

Surprised, she asked, 'Isn't Auckland the place where you and I shall be living?'

'No. I think we should live in Thames. I'd like to see more of Richard, and I'm sure you'd rather be nearer to your parents. Some of us don't have our parents for very long,' he added quietly.

She knew what he meant, but changed the subject by saying, 'Dearest, we have so much to discuss. For instance, after we're married, will you mind if I still keep my business?'

'Of course not. Do you think I'll expect you to give up something you've worked for just because you're married to me? As a matter of fact I've been wondering about Shaw's business, which I presume he'll need to sell. Would you like me to buy it for you?'

The mere thought made her gasp.

Guy went on, 'Running both businesses will require a manager in one of them, but you'll be needing staff in any case. . .especially when you want to remain at home with a baby.'

Linzi's face became a rosy pink as she said, 'My dear one, you *are* looking ahead. I haven't started to think of babies. . .yet.'

He took her into his arms and, looking down into her face, spoke in a low voice. 'I'm looking at our future together. I want you to do whatever makes you happy. There'll be no need for you to work, but I know you're an active person who would prefer to be busy with something constructive rather than frittering away the days.'

She nodded. 'Yes, you're right. I like to be busy.'

'As for the babies, we can make a start on the first whenever you say the word.'

Before she could speak his mouth closed over hers, and as he crushed her against him his need called to her in a loud, clear voice that echoed in the depths of her soul.

It sent her own need into a whirl of passionate desire, causing her to give an involuntary arch against him as an answer to his call. The next instant she was swept up into his arms and carried across the passage to the bedroom, where she was transported into undreamed-of heavenly bliss until she fell asleep in his arms.

Three weeks later Linzi and Guy were married in the small Thames church where they had first met. The reception was held in the same hillside restaurant, and as they sat at the bridal table Linzi turned a radiant face towards her husband. 'I have a strong feeling of *déjà vu*,' she whispered.

'You mean you feel you've done this before?'

'Yes, except that this time you and I are the bride and groom instead of best man and bridesmaid.'

Guy said, 'If you look carefully you'll notice that some people are missing. They've gone to Auckland.'

'The ones I love are here,' she said, sending fond glances towards her parents and her grandmother, who had crossed the Tasman Sea with them and who now intended to live in New Zealand.

He said, 'You're still adamant about not allowing me to buy Shaw's business for you?'

'Definitely. I've thought about it and have decided there wouldn't be enough time to cope with more than the one I already have. Besides, if I become too involved with business I'll have no time to spend painting or to be with my husband and children.'

He leaned towards her to whisper, 'Darling, did I happen to mention that I love you very dearly?'

She smiled happily. 'Yes, but I'd like to hear it again. . .and again.'

At that moment Beatrice Nelson came to stand behind Linzi's chair, and, leaning down, the older woman whispered, 'My dear, you are the loveliest bride I've ever seen. I'm so proud of you.'

Linzi flushed with pleasure then murmured, 'Thank

you, Aunt Bea, but it's only because I'm so—so very happy.'

Bea's face beamed as she went on, 'Richard and I are delighted with the way things have turned out.'

Her words caused Linzi to remember earlier thoughts that had crept into her mind at Kauri Cottage, and now she looked at her aunt with a query hovering on her lips. 'Aunt Bea. . .do you mind if I ask you a question?'

'Of course not, dear. What is it?'

There was a momentary hesitation before Linzi whispered, 'When you asked me to paint the cottage and the pohutukawa tree did you know that Guy would be at the cottage?'

A gurgling laugh escaped Bea. 'Of course I knew, dear. *Why do you think I sent you there?*' Then she added dreamily, 'The two paintings look wonderful in our lounge. They're like a symbol of love.'

Guy caught Bea's last words and as the older woman moved away he murmured to Linzi, 'What did she mean by "a symbol of love"?'

Linzi explained.

Guy smiled as he whispered huskily, 'My darling, I know of a more potent symbol of love. It's the light in your eyes when you look at me. I'll do my utmost to keep it burning.' Then he kissed her tenderly.

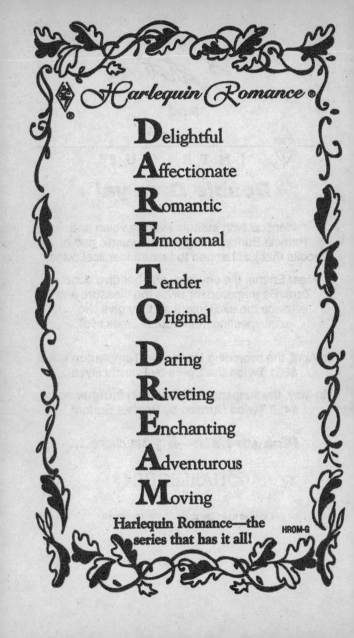

Harlequin Romance®

Delightful

Affectionate

Romantic

Emotional

Tender

Original

Daring

Riveting

Enchanting

Adventurous

Moving

Harlequin Romance—the
series that has it all!

HROM-G

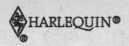
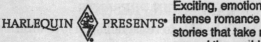
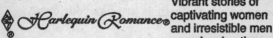

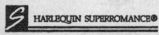

HARLEQUIN PRESENTS®

HARLEQUIN PRESENTS
men you won't be able to resist falling in love with...

HARLEQUIN PRESENTS
women who have feelings just like your own...

HARLEQUIN PRESENTS
powerful passion in exotic international settings...

HARLEQUIN PRESENTS
intense, dramatic stories that will keep you turning
to the very last page...

HARLEQUIN PRESENTS
The world's bestselling romance series!